A VALENTINE WALTZ

"I shan't do anything dangerous at the ball," Amy promised. "I'll merely be an added pair of watchful eyes." A wistful expression settled on her face as she turned and looked into the burning coals.

Hart reached over and turned her chin to face him. "I have said you may help. Why are you now so blue-deviled?"

She played with a fold in the fabric of her white gown. " 'Tis only that this would have been my first ball and I am not allowed to dance."

Wanting to remove the sadness from her face, Hart realized that Miss Reed was playing a waltz. He took Amy's hand. "I have an idea. Come with me."

Amy didn't protest in the least. She knew in that instant she would follow the gentleman almost anywhere.

The baronet led her to the side of the room where they could no longer be seen by the others, then took her in his arms. Very slowly at first they began to waltz around in a small circle. Amy was shocked at the impact of his hand holding hers, the other at her waist. It was as if she felt alive for the first time. His nearness overwhelmed her senses. Their eyes locked; then their movements grew slower and slower, until they stopped completely. The music still flowed around them, but it was as if they could no longer hear anything but the beat of their own hearts in unison . . .

Books by Lynn Collum

A GAME OF CHANCE

ELIZABETH AND THE MAJOR

THE SPY'S BRIDE

LADY MIRANDA'S MASQUERADE

THE CHRISTMAS CHARM

THE VALENTINE CHARM

Published by Zebra Books

THE VALENTINE CHARM

Lynn Collum

ZEBRA BOOKS
Kensington Publishing Corp.
http://www.zebrabooks.com

ZEBRA BOOKS are published by

Kensington Publishing Corp.
850 Third Avenue
New York, NY 10022

Copyright © 2001 by Jerry Lynn Smith

All Kensington titles, imprints and distributed lines are available at special quantity discounts for bulk purchases for sales promotion, premiums, fund raising, educational or institutional use.

Special book excerpts or customized printings can also be created to fit specific needs. For details, write or phone the office of the Kensington Special Sales Manager: Kensington Publishing Corp., 850 Third Avenue, New York, NY, 10022. Attn. Special Sales Department, Phone: 1-800-221-2647.

First Printing: February, 2001
10 9 8 7 6 5 4 3 2 1

Printed in the United States of America

One

A weak December sun struggled to penetrate the blanket of grey clouds streaming across the skies above Basingstoke. The bitter north wind strongly encouraged the local citizens to hurry about their business and not linger outdoors. Despite the inclement weather, the streets of the market town that lay in the north of Hampshire County bustled with people, being the largest borough on the road between the cities of Winchester and London.

An elegant black carriage drew up in front of Needham's, and three disparate females stepped down, entering the linen-draper's shop. Mrs. Vivian Reed, a tall, raw-boned woman with greying brown hair beneath a black bonnet and no pretensions to beauty, led the trio. Despite her rather drab black bombazine dress, Mr. Needham clapped his hands, and several young clerks hurried to the lady. It was well known that the widow spent lavishly on fabrics for her stunningly beautiful daughter, Miss Helen Reed, a blonde goddess who was everything her mother was not.

Mrs. Reed, the only daughter of the late Baron Landry, rarely let anyone ignore her elevated birth. She shooed away the eager young minions in aprons and made her way to the owner, who sat near the glowing coals of a small enclosed grate. "Needham, this is my niece, Miss Amy Addington, newly arrived from her home in Italy. She is to be companion to my daughter and must be properly attired." The lady began to draw off her gloves, then as an afterthought added, "Nothing too bright or too ornate."

Mr. Needham, a rotund fellow with a mop of golden curls more suited to a small child than a middle-aged man, struggled to his feet and bowed to the dark beauty who stood between Mrs. Reed and her daughter. He thought the Reeds' young relation remarkably pretty with her raven black curls dangling from beneath an unfashionable grey bonnet and her warm brown eyes twinkling with a look of good humor and excitement. Still, the young lady was cast into the shade by the golden beauty of Miss Reed.

"Do you speak English, miss?"

Miss Addington gave a nod of her head. "I do, sir, for my father was from Norfolk County, although he left these fair shores nearly twenty-five years ago."

Mr. Needham's face split into a pleased grin. "Then welcome to England, Miss Addington. Have you any preferences for fabrics or color?"

Amy Addington's gaze roved over the rows of draped fabrics in a vast array of colors and textures. Anticipation raced through her breast at the thought of having new material with which to fashion several gowns. For years she'd had to make do recutting old garments of her late mother's for both herself and her sister.

Amy suddenly wished Adriana were with her to enjoy this long-denied treat, but she felt certain that Lady Margaret, who'd invited the elder Miss Addington to Scotland, would be taking good care of her goddaughter. Putting her mind to the task at hand, Amy said, "I should like something in red or blue, sir." Her mother's gowns had often been in somber greys and blacks.

"Very good, miss." With that, the shopkeeper motioned the ladies to follow him as he ambled between the rows. "I've just received a new shipment from the Continent now that Bonaparte has been routed. Mayhap one of these bolts will strike your fancy, Miss Addington." He swept his beefy arm toward stacks of colorful muslins, cambrics, and lutestring fabrics.

Mrs. Reed lifted the edge of a silvery sarcenet announcing, "Too impractical." Then she tossed it aside, choosing instead a simple white muslin with blue dot and pronounced, "Very nice."

Amy fingered the sarcenet with regret, but she knew her aunt correct. Impoverished and working as a companion, she must dress in the more sedate fabrics. Aunt Vivian had been kind enough to employ her for Helen's come-out, but Amy didn't lack sense. She would likely stay on as companion to her aunt and lead a far more secluded life once her cousin had made a brilliant match. Being realistic, Amy knew there was little chance of some gentleman of the *ton* overlooking her straitened circumstances.

Mrs. Reed called to her niece, and Amy hurried to the lady. They quickly became engrossed in the task of selecting just the right colors for the dark-haired young lady. The fashion dictated that unmarried females wear whites and pastels, so Amy found her choices of vivid reds and deep blues vetoed by her aunt in favor of the milder pinks and yellows. Mrs. Reed was quite generous with her niece. While Amy was herself something of a beauty, there was little doubt in the widow's mind that, even at her best, the young lady would in no way distract attention from her daughter's extraordinary looks.

Miss Helen Reed soon grew bored, as the purchases had nothing to do with her. She wandered to another part of the shop, two dazzled young clerks trailing in her wake. The ravishing blonde was quite used to such attention from males, and after some time quite forgot herself and began to chatter with the young men despite her mother's oft repeated warning to remember she was the niece of a baron and not some shop girl.

To Amy, the variety of fabrics selected by her aunt seemed to grow to an unbelievable height. She protested Mrs. Reed's generosity, but that lady reminded her that they were to go to London in the spring, and appearances were everything in Society. It would not do for Helen's companion to appear shabby. Therefore Amy would have need of all the gowns, and they could be made here in Hampshire for far less than in Town.

From across the linen-draper's shop Helen interrupted the discussions of her mother and cousin. "Look, Mama, this ribbon is the exact same shade as my eyes. It would be perfect with my new white crepe gown." The young lady held a length of aqua blue ribbon up beside her heart-shaped face as she turned to her mother. The two besotted young clerks were nodding agreement like moonlings.

Mrs. Reed never took her gaze from the blond lace she was inspecting. "Dearest, I told you this was a shopping trip for your cousin. You already have three shades of ribbon for the dress of which you speak; you have no need for more at present."

Amy stared at her aunt in surprise. She had been with her relatives in Basingstoke for only three short weeks, her aunt having sent funds for her and her sister to journey from Italy, where they had been born and raised by their English father and Italian mother, but in that time it had become apparent that Miss Helen Reed was the apple of her mother's eye. It was rare that the lady did not give in to her beautiful daughter's requests, no matter how absurd.

Helen's lovely cheeks flamed deep pink, but instead of creating a scene she whirled about, showing her back to her mother. Her two devotees murmured softly to her.

Mrs. Reed, absorbed in her present occupation, paid little heed to her daughter's sulks, and soon announced that they had sufficient quantity of cloth and matching trim. She ordered Mr. Needham to send their selections to Stokewood House.

In grand fashion, Mrs. Reed led her party out of Needham's, and they boarded their elegant coach for home. Still in a huff, Helen maintained a frosty silence for the first few minutes, but soon Vivian Reed set about trying to appease her daughter with promises of another visit to the linen-draper's the following week in which she might select whatever she wished. Helen showed no joy at the announcement, only treating it as her due. Within some twenty minutes the women were deposited at the front door of the home which Mrs. Reed had leased on the death of her husband, a London barrister.

Mr. Arthur Reed had achieved only minimal success at his profession—nothing that would have allowed his family to live in their current style. But scarcely a month before his own death, he'd received a large legacy from an old client who'd died childless. There were those clerks in the gentleman's office who swore that Mrs. Reed had nagged her husband into his grave upon learning of the fortune. The lady's incessant demands that they improve their circumstances for the sake of their daughter were rumored to have ruined his health.

On the gentleman's demise, Mrs. Reed had duly left the management of their funds with her husband's partner, sold the small house in Cheapside, and moved her daughter to the village of Basingstoke where they could start anew, living like gentry and accepted by all the best families. Her plan from the beginning was to return to London and introduce her daughter to Society when she turned eighteen.

Stepping down from the carriage upon arrival at

Stokewood House, Amy tugged her too thin woolen cape tighter against the wind. While waiting for her cousin and aunt to descend, she spied a carriage pulled up in front of their own vehicle. Since her sister, Adriana, had departed for Scotland, there had been no guests calling at Stokewood other than the local vicar, and he came by foot. "You have a visitor, Aunt."

Mrs. Reed eyed the vehicle, then quirked one dark brow. " 'Tis my late husband's partner, Jonas Ingram. He manages our affairs. I wonder whatever he can be doing here, for I know he dislikes coming into the country. Perhaps he has at last found a house for us in Mayfair."

The family butler, Bigelow, an aging man with a decided paunch and snow white hair, opened the door for his mistress. He informed her that Mr. Ingram awaited her in the library.

The lady handed her gloves, cape, and bonnet to the servant, then turned to the girls. "Helen, take Amy to your room and show her the latest copies of your *La Belle Assemblee*. Together you can select the styles to show the seamstress when she arrives tomorrow." With that, Mrs. Reed hurried to greet her guest.

The butler took Amy's bonnet and cape, then moved to assist Helen, but the young lady stepped back, merely handing the man her bonnet. "I'm still quite chilled, Bigelow. It's frightfully cold out. I shall keep on my wrap for now. Come, Amy, we shall find just the right styles for you."

Amy followed her cousin upstairs to her room, surprised that her relative would take the time to pick fashions for someone other than herself. In truth, she had come to realize that Helen was more absorbed in her own affairs than truly selfish, but that was Mrs. Reed's fault, for she'd constantly spoken of her daughter's beauty and listed the great rewards to come when Helen made a great match during her Season.

Helen reached out for the handle of her chamber door, but before her hand touched the brass fixture, she seemed to fumble with something. To Amy's amazement, a coil of aqua blue ribbon swirled to the floor at her cousin's feet.

Amy's brown eyes widened. "Cousin, did you . . . take that ribbon your mother said you could not have?"

Miss Reed angrily shook her head. "How dare you call me a thief? That skinny clerk, Luke, gave it to me." She stooped and jerked the aqua satin strip from the floor, stuffing it into her reticule. "He said that anyone so lovely as I should have my every wish."

The young lady thrust open her bedchamber door, then paused. "I'm not in the mood for looking at fashion plates at the moment. We shall do it later." With that, she stepped inside and slammed the door in her companion's face.

Before Amy could move or even think about what she should do, for she must convince her cousin how improper taking gifts from admirers was, a loud shriek echoed in the hall. She recognized her aunt's voice. With little idea as to what she could do to help, she hurried back down the narrow angled stairway to see what disaster had befallen Aunt Vivian.

The library door stood open, and Amy could see her aunt prostrate on a leather wing chair. A bevy of servants, from Bigelow to the upstairs maid, were surrounding the weeping woman, trying to relieve her distress. Standing in front of the fireplace was a gentleman dressed in an unremarkable black morning coat over a plain grey waistcoat with a pristine white cravat tied in a simple knot. His brown hair glistened with oil above a face set in lines of distaste at the scene being enacted before him. Amy surmised this was her aunt's solicitor, Mr. Jonas Ingram.

Mrs Reed wailed, "What am I to do? I'm ruined."

At that moment footsteps sounded behind Amy, and Helen appeared at her side. The ethereal beauty took one look at the situation, then rushed to her mother's defense without the least notion of what had happen. "Mr. Ingram, what have you done to Mama?"

Jonas Ingram sighed, moving away from the busy servants who continued to proffer their mistress water, handkerchiefs, and hartshorn, only to have every offered item rebuffed. Without answering Miss Reed, the gentleman calmly spoke to the butler. "That will do, Bigelow. Mrs. Reed's daughter can see to her needs now."

Despite the gentleman's remark, Helen stood glaring at the solicitor, so Amy went to her aunt as the servants filed out of the library. But the lady was inconsolable, her thoughts as usual dwelling on her daughter. "All my plans shall come to naught. Whatever am I to do with my beautiful Helen now? We shall all end our days in poverty."

Mr. Ingram drew his hands behind his back. " 'Tis not as bad as that, madam. You must simply scale down your plans for a London Season for the girl." His green gaze settled on the beautiful blonde glaring at him before he added, "With her looks, you can fire her off in some smaller locale without the least problem and at half the cost."

Helen's brilliant aqua eyes widened, and she turned to stare at her mother with horror. "What does he mean, Mama? Am I not to go to London?"

Mrs. Reed sniffled into her handkerchief and could only babble while lost in misery. "I've made plans for years. Scrimped to send her to the best school. Borrowed money to hire the best dance instructors. Taken every precaution that she socialize with only the finest families. And it has all gone up in smoke."

Amy's heart went out to her aunt, who'd only shown her kindness since her arrival. It had been evident from her first day at Stokewood that Helen was being groomed for social success. To marry not only wealth, but a title as well. In truth, to achieve everything that Mrs. Reed, despite her connections, had failed to do in her youth.

The solicitor sighed on seeing that Mrs. Reed was still too discomposed to explain matters. "What your mother is trying to say is that the comfortable income that your father left is lost due to a fire in the West Indies. It will be years before the family sees any profits again. You ladies will have to live on a small stipend until then, which means that you must economize."

"What exactly will that entail?" Helen eyed the gentleman warily. She would not easily surrender her long-held dreams of dazzling the *ton* in London.

"No unnecessary purchases, especially new gowns." The gentleman's gaze raked Helen's fashionable pink merino dress. "You will have to give up this large house, but in that I shall be able to help you if you are willing to leave Basingstoke."

Mrs. Reed seemed to come out of her self-imposed misery at that. "Move? Where to?"

The solicitor turned to extend his hands to the flames, avoiding the lady's intense gaze. "I inherited a small house in Bath some years ago—nothing too grand, but I shall gladly allow you the use of the place since I blame myself for making those investments in the Indies."

"Bath." The widow said the word as if seeing how it tasted on her tongue. " 'Tis not as fashionable as it once was, but they have the theater and assemblies in which to present my lovely girl. Yes, that might do."

"But, Mama, there won't be so many eligible earls, marquesses, and dukes to be met in such a city." Helen pouted, but managed to look thoroughly charming.

Mrs. Reed rose, a steely determination in her faded blue eyes. "There will be if we make haste, my girl. We must arrive before Parliament opens in the spring and they all rush back to London." Seeing the disappointment on her daughter's face, the lady patted Helen's cheek. "Don't frown, child, it will only give you wrinkles. Trust that your mama shall see you engaged to some wealthy, titled gentleman by March, or I shall eat my bonnet." With that, she turned back to her late husband's partner. "When can you make the arrangements, Mr. Ingram?"

"This very day."

Amy listened in amazement as Mr. Ingram and her aunt made short work of plans to move the household to Bath. It was soon decided that most of the current staff must be let go, with Mrs. Reed keeping only a butler, cook, footman, and maid to run the smaller establishment in Bath. Helen vehemently opposed the idea of a single maid, since it meant she would no longer have her own personal servant, but her mother quickly silenced her, reminding her that her cousin, Amy, could help fill the void.

Some thirty minutes later Mr. Ingram departed, promising to hire a large cart for the pieces of furniture that wouldn't remain at Stokewood. He promised to visit the ladies once they were settled in their new home. After the gentleman left, Amy urged her aunt to go to the more comfortable drawing room. Once she had the lady comfortably settled, Amy ordered tea while Aunt Vivian lamented the sudden change in circumstances.

They had just started on their simple repast when a knock sounded on the drawing room door, and Bigelow returned, going straight to Miss Addington.

"An express letter has come for you, miss." He extended a silver salver on which lay a missive.

Mrs. Reed craned her neck to see the addressee. "I only pray it isn't more bad news. We have certainly had enough for one day."

At once Amy recognized her elder sister's writing and quickly grabbed the letter. "It's from Adriana."

The widow looked back to her plate of watercress sandwiches. "Well, open it, child. I am anxious to know if my niece arrived in Scotland safely."

Amy broke the wax wafer and unfolded the missive. Into her lap fell the gold necklace with a charm that her sister had worn for years, and a bank draft for one hundred pounds. The bank document was signed by a gentleman of whom Amy had never heard. Despite the check being for more money than she'd ever seen, it was the necklace that drew her immediate attention. She lifted the beautiful medallion etched with a picture of the goddess Minerva that glinted in the candlelight as Amy turned the good luck charm over. Why had her sister sent her the necklace that was so dear? Did it mean what Amy thought?

She quickly read the letter, then looked to her aunt, disbelief etched on her face. "My sister was married on Christmas Day to Viscount Borland! Whoever is that?"

"Borland!" Ambition glowed in Mrs. Reed's eyes as she tilted forward as if to see the words herself. "He is your godmother's grandson and an excellent match, titled and wealthy. I should hope to do as well for Helen. Do they return to London soon? Why, with his connections, my daughter would——"

Amy shook her head, knowing where her aunt's thoughts were leading. "The note says they were to leave on an extended honeymoon in Italy the following day. They don't know exactly when they will return.

She sends her best wishes and promises to invite us to stay with them in London later in the year when they return. She hopes we shall have a delightful Season."

Helen edged closer, eyeing the striking piece of jewelry. "Why did she send you a necklace? Is it a belated Christmas gift?"

Amy held up the golden trinket that spun on the end of a lovely chain. For her family it held so many memories, and her eyes grew moist. "It's a good luck charm which was given to us by our brother Alexander just before he left us in *Roma* to come to England. The people of *Roma* have a special connection with the ancient goddess Minerva. They say she brings wisdom and prudence to the wearer of her medallion. Adriana was to wear this until she found her heart's desire; then she was to give it to me so that I might find mine. Clearly, Lord Borland is her true love."

"And when are we to meet your brother?" Helen took a bite of one of the tiny watercress sandwiches. "We did not have an opportunity to do so when he was here in school."

Amy shook her head sadly. "I cannot say. My sister and I haven't seen him since he left *Roma* nearly eight years hence. He is with the occupation army in France, but we've had no word from him in years. Much has changed in our lives since he went away." And little of it had been for the good.

She had scarcely been fourteen when their English father smuggled his only son out of Italy and back to England, fearful the boy would be conscripted into the French army. In those days their Italian mother had been alive, but too ill to travel, so Amy and Adriana had remained with her and their father. Alexander had bravely left to go to school until he was old enough to join the British to fight Napoleon.

There had been little communication over the years

due to the family having to hide in Italy while under French domination. Amy didn't even know if Alexander knew that both their parents had died. But she wouldn't dwell on such dark news. Instead she would celebrate her sister's wedded bliss, as she hoped her brother would when he returned to England.

Aunt Vivian put aside her empty plate. "Well, my dear, Adriana's news is wonderful, but at present we must begin our preparations for this move to Bath." There was little joy in the hearts of any of the ladies, but each knew they had little choice.

About to follow her aunt and cousin from the room, Amy folded the bank draft and put it in her reticule. She already knew what she would do with some of the money: pay for at least a few bolts of the fabrics her aunt had ordered and could no longer afford. Most of the material would have to be returned. With that decided, she moved to the looking glass and donned the gold necklace. She lifted the charm and gave it a kiss, hoping that she too might experience its good luck and find happiness. On that positive thought, she hurried after her relations to do her part in the move to Bath.

Some three weeks later, the Reed household was ensconced in Bath, albeit not happily in the house that Mr. Ingram had provided. For Amy Addington, who'd lived much of her life in dreary Italian *pensioni,* any home no matter the size was a treat. The drab little structure with a paint-chipped front door was situated in one of the less desirable parts of the once fashionable watering hole, and was a good twenty-minute walk from Sydney Gardens. The old stone house, far smaller than Stokewood, was filled with Mrs. Reed's great oak furniture, leaving the rooms with a cluttered, overstuffed feel.

The widow's concerns about their shabby residence paled in comparison to the difficulties they'd had finding a foothold in what constituted Bath Society. Despite Vivian Reed's efforts of calling on old family friends, they'd only managed two invitations, and neither had borne fruit. Both had been fashionable routs—parties so crowded that neither she nor the girls had met a single person of note in the milling guests. All they had gained for their efforts were bruised bottoms since all the aging old roués had taken advantage of the crush to play the scandalous rake and pinch whatever came to hand.

That rainy morning Mrs. Reed sat reading the society page of the local paper, trying to come up with a plan to advance her daughter's campaign. Amy scoured the front page hoping for news from the Continent about the occupation army as well as the general news of the day, while Helen perused a guidebook of Bath, making intermittent suggestions of where they might visit next.

"I see there is a shop that sells ices on Milsom Street." Receiving no comment from the other ladies, Helen spoke a bit louder. "Shall we walk to Milsom Street to visit the shops?"

Mrs. Reed looked up from the society page. "Remember what Mr. Ingram said, my dear. We cannot afford to squander our funds."

"Even on so simple a thing as an ice?" Helen slammed the guidebook closed, giving Amy a start. She looked up from her reading. Her cousin's stormy countenance warned her she must make an effort to smooth the girl's ruffled feathers before she settled into the sulks for the day. Aunt Vivian had enough to contend with.

"Did you see a lending library in your guidebook, Helen?" Amy folded the paper and smiled at her beautiful relation.

"What does it matter, if we have no funds to pay for books?"

Amy glanced at her aunt, who had also put down her paper and resumed her breakfast with a wary eye on her daughter. "If you don't mind, I shall pay for us to use the library."

Aunt Vivian patted her niece's hand. "My dear, that is most kind of you, but do not waste your funds on anything so frivolous. While we should enjoy such a treat, your money would be better spent elsewhere—say for the subscription fees to the assembly rooms." There was a hopeful look in the lady's eyes.

While the library held far more interest for Amy, she knew the reason they'd moved to Bath was to find Helen a husband. All expenses must go to that aim. "Then we must sign the subscription book at the New Assembly Rooms as well as the Lower Assembly Rooms that your friend's niece, Miss Sanford, was telling me of at Lady Whitford's."

"Excellent." Mrs. Reed beamed at Amy. "Now, I have come up with a plan to increase our acquaintances in Bath. I have decided that you girls must go to Sydney Gardens, for dear Mrs. Sanford tells me everyone does."

"Walk in this weather! Mama, you know I dislike tramping about outdoors. It always leaves one's hair in such disarray and one's boots coated in dust or mud, and remember we have only one maid. She must do the cleaning for the entire upstairs and down, and we would be adding to her work with our dirty shoes. In my opinion it's far too cold to be outdoors, especially to go all the way to the park and back." She peered out the window, then added, "It's raining, and I might catch my death of cold and then where shall we be?" Helen's list of excuses seemed endless.

"Stuff and nonsense, child. I didn't mean for you to dash out in the street this very moment. I mean when the weather is acceptable. We shall see that you are dressed comfortably, and there is nothing like a brisk walk to put the roses in your cheeks."

Helen pouted. "Well, I prefer my roses in a bouquet."

Mrs. Reed gave her daughter a quelling look before returning to her breakfast.

Amy had no objection to an excursion to the park, but she didn't understand what the trip would accomplish. "Aunt, why do you wish us to walk in Sydney Gardens?"

The lady's eyes glowed as she put down her teacup. "Why, to meet other young ladies and gentlemen of your age. I have realized that the problem is that all my friends are older. What we need are for you to meet young people. They are the ones who attend balls."

Amy folded her napkin and laid it upon the white cloth. "But, Aunt Vivian, we cannot simply go up to a stranger and introduce ourselves. It simply is not done."

"I know that, dear. But people meet in the strangest ways. I have decided that what you require is something that will attract attention, but not in a vulgar way, mind you. So I have this morning informed Bigelow that he must find us a pair of frolicsome pups for you to take on your walk. There is only one thing an Englishman likes more than a good horse, and that is a dog."

Helen sat up, a sparkle coming into her aqua blue eyes for the first time since they had arrived in Bath. "Oh, Mama, you have always refused to allow me a pet. I should adore a pair of lovely little dogs to walk in the park, won't you, Cousin?"

Amy smiled at Helen, but in truth she very much doubted that a pair of dogs, no matter how frolicsome, would gain them entry into the homes of the first families. She turned and looked out the window at the cold January storm which had been battering the house for nearly a week. The steady rain appeared to be giving way to sleet as the trees in the tiny rear garden began to glisten with ice. Amy, used to the far more temperate climate of Italy, had been longing for a glimpse of the sun for days. But now she dreaded the idea of the return of fair weather, for then she would be forced to take her cousin to the park and herd dogs about to draw attention to themselves. It simply didn't bear thinking about.

Mayfair on that January night in the winter of 1816 was as quiet as a country graveyard. The streets were nearly empty of carriages, as much of Society had yet to return to Town with the opening of the Season over two months away. Those elite members of the *ton* who remained in London needed an excellent excuse to be out on such a cold, snowy night. Only the most urgent of matters would draw a hearty soul from in front of his fire.

A hackney cab drew up in front of the Home Secretary's town house where light glowed from the windows. One would have little doubt that such an important member of the government would be in Town. A gentleman dressed in an unfashionable black coat and waistcoat was given admittance into Lord Sidmouth's home and then to His Lordship's presence in the library.

Viscount Sidmouth had a long history of government service and was known for his unimpeachable honesty, so the present situation had caused him a great deal of dismay. He rose from his desk to greet his visitor, the Chief Magistrate of Bow Street, Mr. John Ford. One of Sidmouth's numerous duties as Home Secretary entailed overseeing what constituted the police of London. "What have you discovered, sir?"

Mr. Ford moved toward the fire, his shoulders stooped with the weight of the news he carried. Despite his years of effort to run his organization with the same integrity as had its founder, Mr. Henry Fielding, the gentleman knew that scandal loomed. "I have no proof as yet, my lord, but there can be little doubt that the rumors are true. A great many of Bow Street's officers have engaged to entice thieves to steal from the best homes in order to gain the rewards so freely offered by the owners of the stolen objects. I fear that at present there is not a single man I can trust to send to Bath to handle this delicate matter which you have brought to me."

The Home Secretary moved from behind his desk, coming to stand in front of the fire and gaze thoughtfully into the flames. The matter of which Ford spoke involved the theft of several small but extremely valuable articles from two of the finest families of Bath. Both, it seemed, had been taken during parties, leading both Sidmouth and Mr. Ford to believe that the thief was a member of the Quality. Which made the matter all the more delicate.

"I was convinced there was truth in the story that one of the constables brought to me. For that reason I have engaged an old friend to join us this evening. He has offered to go to Bath and investigate the robberies at Lady Whitford's and Lord Rowland's. Since both thefts took place during social events, I thought a member of the *ton* might be best to handle the matter. No hostess would want a Runner lurking about at one of her affairs."

Doubt clouded Mr. Ford's eyes. "I cannot imagine a gentleman who would be willing or capable of handling such a matter with serious intentions. I don't mean to be rude, sir, but this isn't some lark to be done on a wager."

At that moment a knock sounded on the door. The oaken portal opened and the butler announced, "Sir Hartley Ross, my lord."

The Home Secretary moved to greet the man he'd

known since the cradle. "Hart, welcome, and allow me to introduce Mr. John Ford, presently in charge of Bow Street."

Sir Hartley, a tall gentleman whose subdued splendor cast both of the other men in the shade, bowed his head to acknowledge the magistrate. He stood nearly six feet, with broad shoulders and an athletic build. Light brown hair framed a tanned angular face, which moved into a polite smile. "We've met before, sir. The matter of the theft of Lord Bellingham's paintings."

Mr. Ford's face had been fixed in long frowning lines. He doubted any fashionable gentleman would have the skills needed to stay with the long and often boring details that such an investigation required. Thief-taking was a serious business requiring honest, dedicated men. But when Sir Hartley spoke, recognition dawned in Mr. Ford's eyes and a reluctant smile tipped his mouth. "Why, I remember the case well. Your footman—Birdwell was his name—was accused of being the housebreaker at Bellingham House, and you took it upon yourself to prove him innocent. Turned out to be one of Lord Bellingham's maids and her lover."

Lord Sidmouth tilted his head in surprise as he stared at the young man. He'd always known there was more to Hartley Ross than his reputation as an out-and-outer, but this was the first he'd heard of it since the baronet had begun to move in the *ton*. "I knew nothing of this, Hart. One of London's most admired Corinthians is little more than a sleuth-hound. Next thing I know, you'll be wearing a red vest and taking notes on what your friends say."

The baronet laughed, even as he tugged at his cuffs to make certain they were properly positioned. "Gad, sir, not a red vest. Too *outré* for a member of the Four-in-Hand Club."

The gentlemen laughed.

"I got involved in the Bellingham affair because Birdwell was the only one of my footmen who could procure a decent bottle of brandy during the war with France. Owed him something for that."

Having known Sir Hartley his entire life, the viscount knew the matter involved a great deal more than that, but did nothing to dispute his friend's fashionable *ennui*. "Then are you certain you wish to involve yourself in this little matter of which I spoke?"

Sir Hartley's twinkling green eyes held the answer. "Deuced boring in Town at the moment. I'd like to try my hand at finding the blackguard who steals from friends. Besides, my aunt, Lady Ruskin, has been begging me to visit her for ages. She's been taking the cure for her ailments at Bath for the past ten years."

Mr. Ford and Lord Sidmouth exchanged a look which seemed to bespeak agreement to allow one of London's most eligible and fashionable gentlemen to act as their agent in apprehending whomever was stealing *objets d'art* from the wealthy. The magistrate gave Sir Hartley the name of a constable he might trust in Bath, and after some discussion, the gentlemen said their goodbyes.

As his carriage pulled away from Lord Sidmouth's town house, Hart smiled in the darkness. He'd told none of his friends about being involved with helping clear Birdwell the previous year. They would have thought him daft to have paid so much attention to a mere servant, but the fellow had been with his family for years. That little bit of sleuthing had been the first thing he'd done that had truly sparked his interest in years.

At two and thirty, Hart was finding life in Town a dull routine. He'd mastered all of the gentlemanly pursuits and was now considered to be without equal in driving, sparring at Gentleman Jackson's, and pistols at Manton's. Every young cub who arrived in Town was always out to best him, whether it be in the ring, on the road or on the dance floor. One always knew what to expect when one showed up for any event. Fashionable life was a nuisance.

Even worse was the matter of his mother. Her every waking moment since the death of his father three years ago seemed to be spent badgering him to marry, saying there would be nothing boring about raising a family. But the marriageable young ladies of the *ton* reminded him of china dolls in an Oxford Street shop window—pretty, smiling faces, with little of interest inside their empty heads. It wasn't that he wanted a bluestocking, God forbid, but he did want a conversation with a bit more depth than the price of lace or the last scandal. Somehow he didn't see one of these repressed little models of femininity helping him enjoy life.

As the carriage rumbled through the near empty streets of Mayfair, Hart knew that his plans to return to Shropshire to set up a race stable would have to wait. This mission in Bath was too tempting. He suspected he would need to use a delicate touch, especially if it proved to be some younger son of a titled gentleman trying to cover his gaming debts at the expense of others. All Hart knew was that he was looking forward to beginning the game of cat-and-mouse with the thief.

Two

Sir Hartley arrived in Bath some two days after his meeting with the Home Secretary. He'd sent an express letter announcing his arrival to his aunt, the Dowager Countess of Ruskin, but made no mention of the true reason for his visit. The missive explained instead that he simply wished to remove himself from the dreariness of Town in winter for a few weeks.

He stood in the entry hall of Ruskin Terrace drawing off his York tan gloves. His aunt's residence was a large house in Laura Place, and his gaze swept the elegant interior. He took note of the beautiful pieces of expensive statuary and other small items displayed on the japanned tables that lined the blue silk walls. He was struck anew with how difficult his mission would be, for nearly every home in Bath would be thus decorated, since most people liked to display their collected treasures. That made it easy for an invited guest to slip some little article into a pocket or a reticule, for he hadn't ruled out a woman, in the flash of an eye.

As he was informing the butler that his man would arrive later with his bags, Lady Ruskin appeared at the top of the stairs dressed in grey bonnet and cape, clearly having intended to depart. "Hartley, dear boy, we did not expect you so early."

The dowager, a petite woman in her fifties, hurried

down the stairs and embraced her nephew. Pink-cheeked and looking in the prime of health, one could only speculate at her needing to drink of the curative waters, or surmise that they had done Her Ladyship wonders. Her hair was neatly curled under a sheer white cap visible at the front of her bonnet, but the blackness of the lady's locks was so severe that one knew some artificial method was being employed to thwart time's effects.

"I drove my new phaeton." For a Corinthian like Sir Hartley, that explained his early arrival. He eyed her outdoor attire. "Pray, don't let me keep you from any pending appointment, Aunt."

Lady Ruskin bit at her lip with indecision. "I hate being such a dreadful hostess, but I did promise Lady Halifort to meet her at the Pump Room at two. It would never do to offend the marchioness, or we should be struck from her list for the St. Valentine's Day Ball next month, and that, my dear boy, would be social disaster. It is the event of the Bath Season."

Hart lifted his aunt's hand and gave her a gallant kiss. "Cupid would never be so cruel as to leave such a lovely lady at home on his special night."

The dowager laughed, drawing her hand free. "Silly boy, as if I were interested in romance at my age. 'Tis Silas I am thinking of. High time my son thought about setting up his nursery."

"And what of your poor, lonely nephew? Perchance you might entice the lady to include me on her much coveted invitation list." Hart needed entree into all the best homes if he was to catch the thief.

His aunt cast him a curious look. "Strange you say that, for your mother has been lamenting in her letters your indifference to our sex for some time."

"Now, Aunt Roslyn, you know how contrary gentleman are. 'Tis only the specific ladies my mother chose that I objected to. But I have decided to turn over a new leaf. Do you think Lady Halifort will unbend enough to include me on her invitation list for the ball?"

"I shall mention you to the marchioness. Forgive me, but I must go, or I shall be late. Wilkes," the dowager signaled the butler. "Find Lord Ruskin and inform him of Sir Hartley's arrival, and follow his instructions as regards to his baggage."

Some minutes later, the earl strolled down the stairs and greeted his cousin with such a marked lack of warmth that Hart nearly laughed. Giving little thought to her son's dignity, Lady Ruskin ordered him to bring their guest to join her and her friends in a glass of the healthful waters. Without a backward glance, the aging countess exited the house and climbed into her sedan chair to be taken to what was clearly more of a social outing than something that would benefit her health.

Left on their own, the men settled in Lord Ruskin's library to sip glasses of brandy. Hart welcomed the warming liquid after his cold journey. As the earl sank into the opposite leather wing chair, he offhandedly tossed out suggestions for the entertainment of his newly arrived guest. The baronet took the measure of the young man he'd not seen for some time.

At five and twenty, Silas, seventh Earl of Ruskin, had grown handsome with age, having left his spotty face and plumpness behind. One could only wonder about his temperament, for he had been a rather spoiled and vengeful child. Severe boredom showed on his visage, but that was standard for any fashionable buck these days. His dark blond hair, fashioned à la Titus, framed a well-featured face from which peered deep blue eyes. He was slender, yet well-proportioned, but dressed with a fastidiousness that bordered on being foppish.

In Town, Hart often heard Silas's name linked with some notable beauty on the stage or of the demimonde, but there had been no rumors that were out of the ordinary for a wealthy young man of fashion. The fact was the two men held different interests and moved in very different circles, so they rarely met.

Interrupting his cousin's monologue of places to visit, Hart remarked, "I am surprised to find you here in Bath with your mother. Thought you would still be at the family estate in Lincolnshire or back in London."

"Mother hates the country. Hasn't set foot in the castle since Father died, so we've celebrated the holidays in Bath for the past few years. She insists I escort her about to all these boring affairs, at least until the Season opens in London." Ruskin grew silent a moment, then added, "Suddenly she is determined to find me a proper wife."

Hart arched one brown brow. "Thinking of taking the plunge into matrimony so soon?"

"Ain't such a blockhead as to tie myself to some silly chit that wants me to dance attendance on her. Got my own affairs to attend, if you take my meaning. Mother's bound to catch cold at trying to make a match for me, but I don't tell her as much or she'd fly into the boughs, and then there would be hell to pay. The old girl's getting more and more demanding of my time." The earl's mouth puckered into a sulky pout.

Hart knew what his cousin meant. Mothers were the bane of Society, trying either to fire a daughter off or to select the perfect bride for a son. It amazed him that his own esteemed parent had yet to discover that he was bear-led by no one.

For the time being, he had no worries on that point, for his mother was safely with friends in Scotland. He glanced at his cousin and realized the young man was very much a gadabout on the Town without a serious thought in his head. Hart had decided even before he'd arrived not to take Silas into his confidence, should he find his cousin in residence. Perhaps the childhood

memories of the earl as a spoiled bully had unduly in-
fluenced Hart's decision, but he was convinced that the
fewer who knew of his mission, the less likely there
was to be a leak of information. Society lived for gossip, and this news would set the tongues to wagging
should his cousin be indiscreet. Secrecy was the key to
catching this thief. In fact, Lord Sidmouth had been
most insistent on that matter.

All Hart needed to do now was to join in his aunt's
social rounds. With a bit of luck, he would likely be
present when the next robbery took place, even hopefully catch the culprit in the act.

Still a bit chilled from the morning's journey in the
January cold, he moved his booted feet closer to the
warmth of the fire. "Well, while I am here, I shall
gladly escort Aunt Roslyn to any entertainments and relieve you of the task."

Lord Ruskin gave a bitter snort as he rose and thrust
his glass onto the mantel, where the cut crystal nearly
toppled, spilling the remaining brandy. "Kind of you to
offer, but ain't likely the old girl will surrender my company so easily. She's got a Lady Cecilia Murray in mind
for me, and the chit's in Bath until March. But you're
welcome to join us."

Sensing his cousin's pent-up emotions under his
mother's excessive attention, Hart rose. "Perhaps my being here will redirect her thoughts for the time being.
Shall we take a stroll about town? It's been years since
I've visited the place and I'd like to see how things have
changed."

"Would you object if we stop by a gallery on Great
Pulteney Street? The fellow there has a new painting I
should like to view. I'm always looking to add to my
collection." The earl gestured to a beautiful depiction of
the Thatcher Stone near the shores of Torbay.

Sir Hartley looked up and nodded. "Very nice. I have

no objection to where we go as long as it is nowhere near Abbey Square."

"Don't want to go to the Pump Room and be forced to drink those cursed foul waters any more than I, do you?" Lord Ruskin grinned at his cousin.

"Not even if I were dying of thirst," Hart replied. The gentlemen laughed, then went to retrieve their great-coats to walk about the city. The shared jest made Hart think that perhaps his feeling about Silas might improve on closer acquaintance.

Frolicsome and *pups* were not words one would have used to describe the two canines that Bigelow had pro-cured under Mrs. Reed's orders. *Listless* and *mongrels* would be better suited to portray the pair. Coming down the stairs that morning, Amy eyed the two creatures with dismay. Both animals lay sprawled on the worn hall rug as if they'd walked to Bristol and back that very day. The larger one, a scrawny black mutt with a half-missing ear and long nose, had skin so tightly drawn over his frame that it displayed every rib; he appeared to own some hunt-ing hound in his ancestry. He lifted his head and eyed Amy warily. Clearly, the dog had learned that a human was not always a friend.

The smaller animal, a grey pug with a dark face, also looked to be little more than a bag of bones. He lay on his side and watched Amy with alert but cautious black eyes, seemingly trying to decide if she was worth the struggle to roll upright. The little dog sniffed at the air and, appearing to smell nothing of interest on the ap-proaching stranger, stayed where he was.

"Bigelow, has my aunt seen these . . . poor speci-mens?"

The butler shook his head, but crossed his arms over his chest, seemingly fed up with the entire enterprise.

"It's the best I could do with so little time and money, miss. People are strange. I think they'd rather sell their spouse for what I was offering rather than give up their favorite dogs."

Amy was certain she'd never seen two more deplorable creatures. "Are they clean?"

"That is the one thing I am certain of, miss. Had to wash the filthy beasts myself." His aggrieved tone indicated that such a task was beneath him.

"Wherever did you find them?" Despite the black dog's unhealthy appearance, Amy stooped and gently stroked the animal's head, and for her effort got a wag of his tail. On closer examination, she could see that one foot was slightly malformed, no doubt the reason the mongrel was in such poor condition, for he couldn't earn his keep. When large, gentle brown eyes gazed into hers, she knew her heart was lost.

"Well, miss, I—" Bigelow halted his tale when a squeal of delight echoed in the small foyer.

At the head of the stairs, Helen stood with her hands clasped together in elation. "They are here." She dashed down the stairs, the ribbons on her yellow sprig muslin gown fluttering, and went straight to the small pug that struggled upright, then nuzzled his new owner's hand. "Why, they look like they've not eaten in a month, Bigelow. Who could have been so cruel? We should search them out and have them taken to the gaol for such barbaric treatment."

"Now, Miss Helen, 'tis nothin' like that. I don't think they had any owners. You see, there's this eccentric old lady, the widow of some naval hero, who resides in a cottage at the edge of Bath, and she takes in strays that come to her door. Said this pair showed up a week ago from who knows where. Fed them what she could, but with so many animals to take care of, it's too much for her straitened circumstances. She was more than happy to sell 'em to me when I promised 'em a good home."

Helen began to weep in earnest as she drew the little pug to her breast. Amy, realizing that her cousin would fall into a fit of the vapors unless she acted quickly, said, "Cousin, we have no time for tears. Food is the answer to their sad state. Come. Shall we share our breakfast with our new pets?"

Looking up through her tears, Helen nodded. "You are quite right, Cousin."

With that, she rose, still carrying the pug, and they all trooped into the small breakfast parlor. Amy sacrificed most of her buttered eggs and all of her kippers to the black hound who would now forever be her most loyal friend. Helen was equally generous with the pug. As the girls ate toast with marmalade and drank tea, they decided on names for the animals. Helen dubbed the pug Sugar, because she declared him so sweet. Amy chose the name of an old Roman emperor who, despite his sad appearance, had done great things for the ancient empire, Claudius.

The meal did wonders for the two canines. Their outward appearance didn't improve, for that would take weeks of food, but their spirits were so revived that Helen suggested that they take the animals with them on their walk to Sydney Gardens.

Doubtful at first, Amy finally agreed when Claudius upended a chair while chasing Sugar about the small breakfast parlor. The young ladies were soon dressed in their pelisses and bonnets, being dragged down the street to the park by two animals that knew little of leashes and manners.

The winter sun did its best to counter the January chill, and the lack of wind helped make for a pleasant but cold day. The brisk walk kept the young ladies from being uncomfortable in the frosty air. The park bustled with people out enjoying the first nice day in nearly a week, but none were known to Helen or Amy, so they strolled up and down, garnering strange looks at their furry companions.

Then from across the gardens, a voice shouted, "I say, Miss Amy Addington, hello!"

Surprised to hear her name called in Bath where she knew not a soul, Amy looked up to see two fashionable young men hurrying toward her. One was a complete stranger, but the other, a chunky young gentleman with dark red hair, she recognized as Mr. Noel Latham. She and her sister had met him when he'd come aboard the *White Gull* at Lisbon during their journey from Italy. The young man was returning to England after visiting his father.

"*Buon giorno,* Miss Addington." The gentleman bowed, sweeping off his hat, then grinned and continued in fluent Italian. "Are you missing Rome, or have you come to love England as I know you must?" His wandering gaze locked on Helen, and the young man looked as if he'd been struck by a thunderbolt.

Pleased to at last meet someone she knew in this land of strangers, Amy laughed but returned the conversation to English for the sake of her cousin, who had never mastered a single foreign language. "Mr. Latham, how delighted I am to see you in Bath, but I must admit I'm surprised. I thought you were for London."

At the sound of Miss Addington's voice, Latham seemed to awaken from his trance, but his tone sounded distracted. "Decided to spend the winter with family friends here instead." Suddenly he looked about, then inquired, "Where is your lovely sister? I hope she is well."

"Quite well, sir. She is recently married and on her honeymoon in Italy."

Never taking his gaze from Helen, Mr. Latham said

all that was polite about the marriage. To Amy it seemed obvious that Noel Latham was bewitched by her beautiful cousin. His friend, having grown impatient at being ignored, made a noise in his throat as if to remind the young man of his presence.

His cheeks growing pink due to his rude behavior, Latham turned and drew his companion forward. "Where are my manners? Miss Addington, may I present Lord Malcolm Holmes, my oldest friend and the youngest son of the Duke of Holmsby. I am staying with his family in Bath until the London Season."

Lord Malcolm stood half a head taller than Latham, but his build was lean and lanky. Despite expensive tailoring, his grey morning coat hung loosely on his slender frame. Brown locks neatly framed a long angular face, and large hazel eyes peered at the ladies with curiosity. He stepped forward and took Amy's hand, the one without the dog leash, and pressed a kiss upon her kid gloves; then his gaze, too, moved to Helen. "And your lovely companion?"

"Gentlemen, may I present my cousin, Miss Helen Reed."

Having been quietly surveying the two men, Helen saw little to make her heart beat faster, for one was so round, the other so thin, and neither was very handsome, but she well knew what was expected of her by her mother. After politely greeting both gentlemen, she turned her attention to the titled man. She dimpled up at him and fluttered her lashes. "Lord Malcolm, pray can you tell me what entertainments there are to be had here, since we are quite new to Bath?"

But before the young man could answer, a large grey cat sauntered out from behind a cluster of bushes, then froze in horror at the sight of the two dogs resting at the ladies' feet. Both Sugar and Claudius knew their job and lunged at the terrified feline. They commenced to bark and sent the cat straight up the nearest birch tree without a backward glance.

Sir Hartley surmised that little had changed in Bath since his last visit. It was a lovely town thanks to the architect, John Woods, the Elder, who introduced the Palladian-style buildings in the early eighteenth century. But the spa city was well past its zenith as a fashionable site, having been invaded by far too many wealthy Cits and Mushrooms. Still, Hart enjoyed strolling up and down the rolling hills of the beautiful city. The baronet and his cousin stopped briefly and examined the aforementioned painting, but Silas decided it wasn't anything he wished to own, being a rather dreary depiction of the Scottish Highlands during winter. So the gentlemen set out once again to savor the day.

They arrived at Sydney Gardens, where Lord Ruskin encountered an old school friend, Mr. Richard Thornton. A discussion about the latest scandals of the royal family soon followed, mainly the rumor that Princess Charlotte had fallen in love with a penniless German prince and a formal announcement was expected any day. Then talk turned to which horse would be the next darling of the racetrack, each gentleman having already picked a favorite.

To the gentlemen's left, a sudden din of barking attracted their attention. Two of the most disreputable-looking dogs Sir Hartley had ever seen appeared to have cornered something in a tree and were resisting the urging of two young ladies to cease and desist their raucous conduct.

Lord Ruskin lifted his quizzing glass to inspect the scene. "I say, ain't that Holmes with the ladies? Met him and his friend at the Pump Room last week. The duke's son is your kind of gentleman, Hart. Fashions himself a notable whip."

Sir Hartley made no comment, for nearly every young buck in London thought himself a notable whip, and there were barely a dozen he would consider even tolerable. But when a man was a member of the Four-in-Hand Club, everyone tried to impress him with their skills, yet few rarely succeeded.

The ladies at last got control of their animals and, with the gentlemen in tow, drew the dogs away from the tree, allowing its frightened occupant a reprieve. The direction the departing quartet and the dogs took led them straight toward Sir Hartley, Lord Ruskin and Mr. Thornton.

Able to see the women full of face, the earl gasped, then took a half step forward. "I say, would you look at that? Why, the girl in yellow is a stunner. I've never seen her equal even in London. Know who she is, Dicky?"

Mr. Thornton lifted his own glass. "Too far away to be certain." Then he fell silent as the party came closer.

Hart casually surveyed the two females leading their skinny dogs from the park. He agreed with his cousin that the girl in yellow was breathtaking. Guinea-gold curls clustered round a heart-shaped face with flawless porcelain cheeks that were flushed a slight pink in the cold air. Large aqua-blue eyes gazed about with wide-eyed innocence, and her rose-pink mouth was delicately shaped and revealed even white teeth. One would describe her as a goddess, a true Venus in the flesh. She personified the ideal English beauty.

His gaze then moved to the taller woman. Dark and exotic-looking with high cheekbones and almond-shaped eyes, her ivory skin was a shade darker than her friend's. Doe-brown eyes were thickly lashed, but it was the young lady's delectable mouth that drew his attention. Wide, full and sensuous, those shapely lips begged to be tasted. That thought startled Hart, for he wasn't much in the petticoat line and did not rhapsodize about females as a rule. Still, despite his sporting interests, he'd had a few mistresses over the years, but had always been discreet and never pursued the high flyers that his cousin preferred.

Hart knew most men would consider the raven-haired young lady beautiful but not a dazzler like her companion. In truth, he didn't know what it was about her that stirred his blood. All he knew was that at the moment he didn't have time to be bewitched by some unknown female.

The women and their companions continued on their chosen path as the three gentlemen surveyed them in silence. Hart surmised that the brunette was some kind of companion or poor relation. Her plain grey attire was not in the first stare of fashion as was the blonde's yellow ensemble.

Mr. Thornton, after a long, thoughtful look through his quizzing glass, announced, "Don't know the little angel. Why not let Lord Malcolm present her?"

With that pronouncement, Lord Ruskin and Mr. Thornton moved to intercept the advancing ladies, gentlemen and dogs. Hart trailed behind, with little true interest in meeting the ladies no matter their fine looks. He was not in Bath to raise the hopes of matrimony-minded females—if these ladies were even genteel, which one could never be certain of in Bath.

To the baronet's dismay, Lord Ruskin opened the conversation with him as bait. "Ah, Holmes, I wanted you to meet my cousin, Sir Hartley Ross, who has at last accepted our invitation to Bath."

Lord Malcolm's hazel eyes widened and his mouth fell open to be meeting such a famous Corinthian; then remembering himself, he bowed. "Sir Hartley, I'm truly honored. I saw you drive against Lord Brockman at the impromptu carriage races at York last summer. Finest bit of driving I've ever witnessed."

Ruskin brushed aside the compliments to his cousin. "Pray, won't you present us to your companions?" His gaze was riveted on the little blonde who giggled and smiled at them.

The introductions were quickly made, but Hart found he had little chance to become acquainted with either female. He was besieged with questions from the aspiring whip. Giving the appearance of listening to young Holmes's chatter about recent races, the baronet watched as his cousin insinuated himself with Miss Helen Reed with as much skill as a man twice his age.

Miss Amy Addington eyed the three gentlemen with interest, knowing her aunt would be delighted at their good fortune. But there was no guarantee that this chance encounter would advance their efforts, because single gentlemen did not entertain. Since her cousin was the center of attention, Amy stood quietly observing the gentlemen's response. Mr. Thornton and Lord Ruskin openly flirted with Helen. There could be little doubt that the girl's beauty was going to be a great draw.

Then Amy realized that while all the others might be enchanted with Helen, Sir Hartley Ross was not, for he stood back with Holmes and watched the group, an amused expression on his rugged face. Perhaps it was that he was older and wiser, or that Helen's silly giggles did little to attract him, but he showed none of the signs of complete bewitchment that were etched on the faces of the other men.

Strangely, she found the baronet the most interesting of the three men. As she analyzed her feelings of attraction, she suspected it was his reserved and mature mien that she liked. Here was no silly young man toppled by one glance at a pretty face. Or maybe she was female enough to simply admire the rakish set of his black beaver hat over his bright green eyes. There was no denying that he was attractive, but not in the same striking manner as his cousin. Under the baronet's buff greatcoat, he was sedately dressed in dove-grey morning coat, figured grey waistcoat and pale grey buckskins with black Hessians. He was not overly fashionable like Lord Ruskin, whose pale green coat over a yellow waistcoat worked with green leaves and buff pantaloons made one stare in awe.

As Amy's gaze moved up over the baronet's athletic form to his rugged face, her brown eyes met jade-green ones. Her cheeks warmed at having been caught so openly staring. With a determined effort she turned her attention back to the conversation of Helen and her admirers. But as Amy watched and listened, she remained aware of Sir Hartley's presence. Forcing herself to concentrate on her cousin, Amy was surprised at how silly Helen appeared as she babbled on. Even more surprising, the gentlemen seemed to hang on every word of her inane chatter. All present were soon aware that Miss Reed was living with her widowed mother in a house on Forester Road. That the young lady's late father had been a barrister in London. And that her cousin had recently come to be her companion.

Someone touched Amy's sleeve, and she looked up to see Noel Latham. He drew her aside. In whispered Italian, he said, "I think I should warn you that Lord Ruskin has something of a reputation with females. Holmes introduced me to him last week; then later he regaled me with tales of the man's conquests. Seems to go after the most beautiful women of the stage."

"But Helen is a gentleman's daughter. Surely he would never cross the line of what is proper." Wanting to keep their conversation private, Amy also spoke in Italian.

Noel shrugged even as he glared at the earl. "I cannot say, for I don't know the fellow well enough to judge. All I would suggest is that you not allow her to encourage the man."

Amy looked sideways at Mr. Latham. She suspected that jealousy was very hard at work in the young man's chest. Still, she would heed his warning. The Earl of Ruskin could certainly look much higher for a bride than an impoverished beauty.

On the other side of the group, Sir Hartley grew impatient with Silas's flirting and Miss Reed's simpering. While the young lady possessed an outstanding beauty, she appeared much like all the young females of Hart's acquaintance in London. He turned his attention to Miss Addington, who stood in whispered conversation with Holmes's friend, Mr. Latham. Earlier there had been that brief moment when their eyes had met and Hart thought some spark of kindred souls had passed between them; then she'd looked away without acknowledging such, leaving him to think he'd imagined it.

Curious about what the pair were speaking of so intently, he strained to hear their words. To his amazement, he discovered they spoke in rapid Italian, a language of which he had only the most rudimentary skills. Intrigued, he excused himself from Holmes and moved toward the pair, who grew silent at his approach.

"Miss Addington—such an English name for a young lady who speaks Italian as well as a Montague or Capulet."

She smiled, and something strange took place in the baronet's chest.

"My mother was Italian, sir, my father English, and I was born and reared in Tuscany and later Rome. But I would say that since both families of whom you speak were created in the mind of the Englishman Mr. Shakespeare, I doubt very much if they were fluent in Caesar's language."

Hart laughed, liking the twinkle in the lady's warm brown eyes. "Most certainly you are correct, Miss Addington." He then turned to Mr. Latham. "And you, sir. How come you to be so fluent? I would swear you speak far better than schoolroom instruction."

The red-haired man nodded. "My father is a diplomat, sir. We were two years in *Roma* before Napoleon's troops invaded in ninety-nine. I had the advantage of an Italian nurse until I was sent to Harrow." Even as Miss Addington's friend answered the baronet's question, his eyes strayed to Miss Reed in conversation with the earl. Latham frowned.

"So you both have lived in Italy," Hart said. "You must find the English winters very different."

The young lady answered, "I cannot deny that I often miss the sunshine, but there is so much new for me to see that I find I'm not melancholy for my old home."

Hart liked her open-minded sentiments, for many a young miss would be pining for the familiarity of her former life. "And have you seen our Roman ruins? But then, no doubt they must pale in comparison to the real Rome."

Miss Addington smiled, and Hart's instincts warned him to be wary. This woman owned something special. He couldn't put his finger on it exactly, but she was not the usual Society female.

"My cousin and I have only just arrived in Bath and have yet to visit any of the sites. I fear Helen is not a great lover of antiquities. But I believe that every town has something unique that makes it special, and I'm looking forward to seeing Bath's."

About to offer to show her the town, Hart reminded himself he wouldn't have the time for such a pleasant distraction. Just then Miss Reed, Lord Ruskin and Mr. Thornton moved to join them.

The blonde beauty stooped to pick up her pet and fussed over the animal. "Amy, I think we must leave. My little Sugar is beginning to shiver from the cold, aren't you, little one?"

Mr. Thornton arched one brow as he stared at the scrawny animal. "Dashedly ugly little thing. If you don't mind me saying so, the only thing that might help that mongrel would be to put him to bed with a shovel—and that one, too." He gestured to the dog at Miss Addington's feet and then guffawed.

Hart noted that both young ladies' cheeks flamed pink in anger. No matter the wretched creatures' looks, they clearly had the ladies' affections. Miss Addington lifted her chin defiantly. "They are strays that we have only just taken in, sir. I assure you that within a fortnight they will look more the thing. Come, Helen, we must go."

Miss Reed glared at Thornton, then gave a defiant toss of her head, making golden curls bounce. "Come, Sugar, we must go home, and I shall give you a treat." The little dog licked the young lady's face as if he understood.

Lord Ruskin stepped forward and offered to escort the ladies. Miss Reed fluttered her aqua eyes at him, but before she could accept, Miss Addington tucked her arm in her cousin's and tugged her away. "I thank you, sir, but Mr. Latham offered his services earlier."

The look of surprise on the young man's face told Hart the lady was telling a whisker.

Latham gamely cleared his throat. "That I did." With that, he and Lord Malcolm fell into step with the departing ladies.

As Hart, his cousin and Mr. Thornton stood watching the ladies and gentlemen leave the gardens, Silas snapped, "That's a damned loose tongue you have, Dicky. Offended Miss Reed about those cursed mongrels."

Thornton shook his head. "Well, have you ever seen an uglier or sorrier pair of hounds?"

"Of course not, but that's not the point. It's bad manners to say such a thing. It's nearly as bad as telling someone their child looks like a fox or some such slur, even when it's true."

The two friends fell to arguing in earnest. At last Hart had had enough. He suggested they go for a tankard of ale to a nearby inn, and informed the gentlemen that they might never see the females again since they didn't know if the chits moved in the first circles of society.

Silas seemed much struck by his cousin's statement. He slapped his friend on the back and put their dispute to rest. Hart assumed that any further thoughts regarding Miss Reed by his cousin were over. But just for a moment the thought flashed in his mind that he would regret not seeing the dark-haired beauty who spoke Italian.

Mr. Latham and Lord Malcolm escorted the ladies to their front door, making no comment about the state of the neighborhood or their shabby home. The young ladies thanked the gentlemen, then hurried into the house, coaxing their furry friends up the steps. The butler, standing ready to take their coats and bonnets, informed them that Mrs. Reed was awaiting them in the rear drawing room.

The widow sat at a small rosewood desk penning a letter as the door opened. She looked up, smiling, but her face twisted into a mask of disgust when she saw the two animals that bounded into the room. At last finding her tongue, she demanded, "Where did those wretched creatures come from? Tell me you did not parade about the park with two such flea-infested specimens as that."

"Mama, how can you say that? They are not flea-bitten in the least, only half starved, which we have begun to take steps to remedy." Helen went to a blue damask chair near the fire and pulled the shawl from the back of the chair. She wrapped Sugar like a baby. "Besides, we have had great success at the park today. Tell her, Amy."

"We met five eligible gentlemen this morning."

Forgetting all about the dogs, Mrs. Reed turned to her niece. "You did nothing improper to bring about this meeting, did you?"

Wounded by her aunt's remark, Amy moved to stand near the flames as well. Claudius curled at her feet on the rug. "I may have grown up in Italy, but I know how to properly conduct myself, Aunt."

Realizing she'd wounded the girl's feelings, Vivian Reed said, "Please forgive my careless tongue, my dear. I am just so worried that one false step will ruin all our plans. How did this meeting occur?"

Appeased, Amy said, "An old acquaintance of mine, Mr. Noel Latham, came along and introduced us to the Duke of Holmsby's younger son, and he, in turn, presented us to the Earl of Ruskin, his cousin, Sir Hartley Ross, and a gentleman named Thornton."

A look of sheer delight appeared on her aunt's angular face. The lady rose and came to the girls, pressing a kiss on each of their cold cheeks. "Lord Ruskin! You have done well, my dears. I feel certain that this is an omen that our luck is changing. We shall soon have invitations pouring in to the finest parties. In the meantime, I suggest we attend the concert tonight. Shall I ring for tea to warm you up?"

"Oh, yes, Mama, and have Cook send some little sandwiches as well. Sugar is starved."

The widow's gaze lit on the pug, but even his sad appearance could not dampen her delight at the girls' success. She made no comment, merely went and summoned Bigelow to give him instructions.

Amy stared into the fire while Mrs. Reed questioned her daughter about the gentlemen. With a sigh, Amy remembered the warning that Mr. Latham had given her about the earl. She felt that perhaps she should forewarn her aunt not to pin her hopes on that gentleman, at least. "I think I should tell you that my friend Mr. Latham informed me His Lordship's reputation is one of a notorious rake."

"A rake!" Aunt Vivian laughed. "All the better, my dear, since such gentlemen can rarely resist beautiful women, and few can rival my Helen." The lady patted her daughter's arm and beamed proudly.

"But Mr. Latham thinks the earl's intentions toward her may not be honorable." Amy could see that her aunt simply didn't understand the danger.

"Not honorable? He is a titled gentleman, Amy. Such a one would never dally with an innocent girl. It simply isn't done. Now, no more of this nonsense. Helen, when next you meet Lord Ruskin, you must do all in your power to enchant him."

"Yes, Mama."

Amy could see it was useless trying to convince her aunt that dangerous rakes and rogues abounded in the *ton,* even titled ones. It would be up to Amy to watch out for her cousin.

Tea arrived and the ladies began to speak of other matters, such as what to wear to the public concert that evening. Amy suddenly wondered if they would see any of the gentlemen from Sydney Gardens at the theater. She realized that there was very much a part of her that wanted to see Sir Hartley again despite the risk of exposing Helen to the earl's company.

Amy didn't know for certain that Lord Ruskin was anything other than what he seemed, but clearly Mr. Latham, who appeared an honest young man, had some reservations. She only knew that she was determined to keep a watchful eye should they again encounter the earl and Sir Hartley. As for the latter gentleman, until she knew more about Ruskin, she wasn't about to do anything so foolish as to fall for his handsome relative.

"Do you suppose the little beauty from the park will be at Lord Guildford's rout-party this evening?" Lord Ruskin stood in front of a cheval glass beside the door, tweaking his blond curls into perfect symmetry about his handsome face.

Hart looked up from the letter he was reading from the local constable. Lord Sidmouth had told him Mr. Henry Baker could be trusted, and Hart wanted to meet him on the morrow. "I cannot say, but why are you so fascinated with Miss Reed? I believe beautiful women are nothing new to you."

Silas, at last satisfied with his hair, turned his attention to the folds of his cravat. "The chit is ravishing. Or are you so sporting mad you never pay attention to such things?"

"I am able to distinguish between a horse and a woman. I just always prefer a horse since they are less trouble. I would suggest you learn a little more about Miss Reed before you become too enamored. Aunt Roslyn might object to your offering for a veritable nobody when she has a wealthy and titled lady like Lady Cecilia in mind."

The earl turned and stared at his cousin with surprise. "Who said anything about making an offer of marriage to Miss Reed? I have something entirely different in mind."

Hart was shocked to his very core at his cousin's heartless words, but he got no opportunity to voice his opinion before his aunt entered the room saying they must hurry or they would be late.

As they made their way to the Royal Crescent, Hart's thoughts returned to the women they'd met in Sydney Gardens earlier that day. The pair hadn't a footman, but then the rules in Bath had always been more lax than in London. However, he'd gotten the distinct impression, by her look as well as demeanor, that Miss Addington was acting as a protector or companion to her cousin. Whatever their situation, Hart knew he didn't like the idea of his cousin ruining an innocent female. And so he would tell him at the first opportunity.

Three

A night at Lord Guildford's home rendered no clues as to the identity of the Bath thief for Sir Hartley. The company was light, giving the baronet the opportunity to circulate through the rooms, but he saw nothing suspicious. Or perhaps the thief had found nothing worth taking. In truth, the viscount's taste in collectibles left something to be desired. No gold vases, jeweled chalices or ornate snuff boxes were to be seen. Instead the gentleman owned an odd assortment of ancient stone gods and goddesses from a variety of extinct cultures, as well as great chunks of time-ravaged Roman statues excavated from around Bath. Hart could only assume that if the thief attended Guildford's affair, he likely feared injuring himself should he try to lift one of the monstrous pieces of bric-a-brac. It would be difficult to sneak about with a veritable boulder in one's pocket.

The baronet returned home that evening in decidedly dejected spirits. In London the task had seemed possible, but tonight he realized that one man alone had little chance of being at the exact right place at the right time. He would speak to the local constable about finding trustworthy men to pose as servants in the likeliest houses to be robbed. They would be able to help a great deal.

The following morning the baronet rose early for the

meeting with the constable, Henry Baker. Sir Hartley hoped to learn if there had been any new robberies in town. It was the height of the Bath Season, and numerous private parties were held nearly every evening. He entered the breakfast parlor, then stopped at the threshold, surprised to see Silas seated at the table enjoying a hearty meal of gammon and eggs.

"Cousin, I didn't think to find you out of bed so early after such a late night."

Lord Ruskin put down his cup of coffee, then yawned before he said, "Haven't any delectable female to keep me from my slumbers . . . at least not yet. Besides, I've an appointment with my steward. Thanks to Mother's determination to keep me in Bath, the fellow must journey all the way from Lincolnshire to keep me informed about all matters on my properties."

Hart, being rather sharp set, made no comment, but went to the sideboard to fill his plate. He was glad to know that Silas took his responsibilities about his estate seriously. His father had been a conscientious landlord and had left his affairs in excellent state. It was good to know that despite the earl's enthusiasm for his pursuit of beautiful ladies he still took an interest in the welfare of his tenants.

Thinking of Ruskin's paramours reminded Hart that he wanted to speak with the young man about his declaration of the night before. "What exactly are your intentions toward Miss Reed?"

The earl leaned back and stared at his cousin. "Damme, if you don't sound like the girl's father, Cousin."

Sitting down, Hart shot a stare back at Silas. "The girl is of little interest to me except as she may affect our family's good name." In fact, he knew that wasn't the whole truth. Strangely, he didn't want Miss Addington's position threatened by his cousin's randy ways, and there could be little doubt that she would be turned off if she failed to protect Miss Reed, no matter that she was a relation. With that in mind, he tried to clarify his meaning to the earl. "Ruining a delicately bred female will put you beyond the pale, my boy, no matter your title and wealth. You would find yourself—perhaps not a pariah, but very unwelcome in *good* Society, since you can be certain that you will set the tongues of Bath to wagging."

Silas shifted uncomfortably in his seat. "Well, I ain't going to rush out and ravish the chit, if that's what you've gotten in your head."

"What exactly do you intend?"

There was a long moment of silence. Hart wasn't certain if it was because Silas didn't know what he wanted, or knew and was sure that his cousin would disapprove. At last Lord Ruskin angrily pushed back from the table and went to stare out the window.

Keeping his back to the room, Silas snapped, "You know as well as I, Hart, that a penniless girl with no connections, no matter her looks, can expect little better than an offer from some gentleman farmer here in Bath."

"And what is wrong with that? Even gentleman farmers must marry."

Silas turned to face his cousin, horror etched in his handsome features. "Then let them marry the ugly ones who cannot bring decent fellows up to scratch. The thought of Miss Reed's beauty wasted on some clodpole makes one ill. Why, 'tis likely she'd spend her life little better than a milkmaid with a passel of brats hanging on her skirts, that gorgeous face squandered on some bumpkin that don't appreciate what he's got. She's a work of art, and I must possess her."

Hart shook his head, then picked up his knife and fork to eat his meal. He mustn't be late to meet Constable Baker. "You think offering Miss Reed a slip on the shoulder is far better than her being a respectable farmer's wife?"

"Well, *I* certainly wouldn't have her out milking cows. She'd have every luxury and elegance." Seeing the frown still on the baronet's face, Silas huffily added, "You know I won't force the chit to become my mistress, Hart. She can say either yea or nay and I'll not act the cad."

"Pray, have the decency to stay away from her altogether if you don't intend to make her an honorable offer."

The earl went rigid with indignation. "Stay out of my affairs. She wouldn't be the first female to choose a life of ease over one of hard work with few rewards, and you've no right to be interfering in my life, or hers either, for that matter."

With that, the young lord stormed from his breakfast parlor. There was no denying that Lord Ruskin had spoken the truth. There were many like the notorious Harriet Wilson and her sisters who had been impoverished gentry and chose to use their charms to provide income over the more respectable choices. Still, Hart knew it was a hard life for a woman to always know she would be shoved aside whenever a protector grew tired of her favors. No sensible woman would make such a choice.

He rose from the remnants of his breakfast and went to the window, staring out at the small, winter-ravaged garden, the rosebushes pointing stark branches at the sky as if in accusation about their state. He'd overstepped his bounds in taking Silas to task, but he was certain that Aunt Roslyn would never show her face in Bath Society if word spread that her son had ruined a genteel young lady, no matter the girl's modest circumstances.

The clock on the mantelpiece chimed the hour, and

Hart realized he had no time to waste. The meeting with Baker was set some thirty minutes hence at a small out-of-the-way inn on the outskirts of Bath since secrecy was of the utmost importance.

Some ten minutes later Hart tooled his curricle through the hilly streets of Bath. Somehow his worries always seemed less when he was behind a well-matched team, and today was no different. Traffic was heavy with the early morning influx of farmers and milkmaids coming to sell their wares, but the baronet moved in and out of the congestion with ease. Forced to slow at one crossroad, his gaze settled on a particularly pretty milkmaid with heavy pails suspended from a wooden yoke on either side of her. The sight of her worn expression brought back his conversation with his cousin. Why, the idea of Miss Reed as a milkmaid was ridiculous, merely his cousin's means to justify his coming actions.

Frustration settled deep in Hart's chest. He'd changed nothing, other than to make his cousin angry with him. Clearly, one couldn't reason with Silas when it came to his pursuit of a beautiful woman. Perhaps the answer would be to warn Miss Reed. Hart's mind flashed on the beautiful but flirtatious eyes of the beauty, and he suspected that the lady's understanding was not great. Even if she were smart enough to grasp the matter, she might be so determined to snare a title that she wouldn't heed his warning, thinking she could capture Silas's heart and then a wedding ring.

Then the vision of a pair of intelligent brown eyes came to Hart, and he knew what he must do. He would seek out Miss Addington. Once she knew the truth, certainly she would be able to convince her cousin that Lord Ruskin had no intention of marrying beneath his station. Or at the very least, the girl's mother would take precautions to keep Miss Reed from harm.

* * *

The ladies in the house on Forester Road awoke to a bevy of floral tributes to the beauty of Miss Reed. Helen eagerly rummaged through the bouquets on the hall table, calling out the names inscribed on the cards. At last she squealed with delight and lifted a large offering of yellow hothouse daises.

"He sent the largest one."

Mrs. Reed, coming down the stairs to break her fast, asked, "Who, dear?"

"Lord Ruskin, Mama. I think I should very much like to be a wealthy countess."

"What does he say?" Amy asked as she noted her cousin's smile fall away as her mouth moved silently while she read the card.

"He cannot come to Sydney Gardens today due to business, but hopes to see us there on the morrow."

Seeing her daughter's face, Vivian Reed observed, "You must look on the bright side, my dear. You can rest today and be at your prettiest in the morning. In truth, his delay may prove to be an excellent opportunity for you to join me at the Pump Room and see some of my old friends this afternoon. They are quite fixtures there and are acquainted with all the best people. One never knows what may happen with the right introduction."

Helen bit at her lower lip a moment, then said, "I think that an excellent notion, for as Amy said, 'tis the ladies that issue the invitations."

The widow tucked her arm into Helen's, and mother and daughter went to the breakfast parlor in high alt at the notion of seeing Ruskin on the morrow. Amy remained behind, looking at the variety of flowers abandoned on the table. All the gentlemen from the park save Sir Hartley had sent offerings to her cousin. There was a brief moment of satisfaction in that fact for Amy; then she banished the thought as unkind. About to leave, she spied her name on a card tucked in a cluster of small pink tea roses at the back of the table. With trembling fingers she lifted the vellum and turned it over. Disappointment raced through her when she read Noel Latham's name in gold lettering. Suddenly she was ashamed of herself. She should be grateful for her friend's kindness instead of wishing the flowers had come from a certain green-eyed gentleman.

Determined to put the handsome baronet from her mind, she hurried into the breakfast parlor. "Aunt Vivian, if you intend to accompany Helen to the Pump Room, would you object if I should walk out to Mrs. Jones's cottage and see if there is aught I can do to help her?"

Mrs. Reed looked up from her plate. "Who is Mrs. Jones?"

Amy stepped to the sideboard and filled her plate, explaining over her shoulder. "She is the kind lady who sold Bigelow the dogs. He says she collects stray animals and takes care of them. I thought perhaps I might make a donation of some time and a few coins to help her."

"You intend to give the woman more money!" the widow snapped, then realized that without her niece's kindness and funds, they would not have been able to afford to subscribe to the assembly rooms and the concerts. "Well, my dear, you may do as you wish, but I should think you could find something better to do with the funds you have remaining. Remember, it might be some time before Lady Borland returns from her honeymoon to replenish your finances, and I don't know when I shall be able to pay you for helping me with Helen."

"Don't worry about that, Aunt Vivian. I am delighted

to do what I can to help my cousin." Yet Amy knew her aunt spoke the truth about her financial situation. She must not squander the funds her sister sent her. But she'd grown up in a household with tightened circumstances and well knew what even the smallest amount of help might do for Mrs. Jones. In truth, very little of the one hundred pounds had been used. "I promise I won't be overly generous, Aunt."

With a sigh, Mrs. Reed gave in rather ungraciously. "Well, 'tis your money after all. You may toss it to the four winds if you like, but I hope you will not."

Turning to her cousin, Amy inquired, "I shall go immediately after breakfast. Would you like to accompany me, Helen? We can be back long before you are to go with your mother."

The young woman looked up from feeding Sugar a bit of ham under the table. "Will there be anyone of worth to be met there?"

Amy laughed. "I believe the only males to frequent Mrs. Jones's home are the four-legged furry type."

Helen shook her head. "I must walk in the cold on the morrow for good purpose. Today I shall stay home and keep warm with Sugar until I go with Mama. Pray thank Mrs. Jones kindly for having let Bigelow buy our pups."

Mrs. Reed's face puckered in distaste. "If you insist on going, Amy, make certain you take the maid with you."

"Not the maid, Mama, the footman. I shall need Molly to mend my pink walking dress. It has a tear from the last time I wore it, and I should like to have it ready for the morning."

About to offer to do the mending, Amy pressed her lips together. She was afraid the task might just be the first of many that her aunt would use as an excuse to keep her from going. If Molly hadn't found time to do the mending, Amy would do the job when she returned.

She finished her breakfast, then darted up from her seat and hurried to the door. "I shall take Peter, and we won't be gone very long, Aunt." With that, she hurried from the room to retrieve her coat and bonnet.

After receiving exact directions from the butler, Amy, Claudius and the footman set out to find Mrs. Jones's small cottage and her collection of stray animals. The morning was cold yet sunny, but keeping at a brisk pace, the trio suffered little from the effects of the chill wind. The gold good luck charm she'd received from her sister bounced about at her throat. She reached up to capture it, wondering about her sister's new husband. Amy couldn't wait to meet the man who'd captured Adriana's heart, but it would be months before that happened. In the meantime she would do her best to help Helen win her heart's desire.

As they hurried past Sydney Gardens, Amy's thoughts returned to the meeting with all the gentlemen the day before. A good beginning in Helen's pursuit of happiness. Remembering Noel Latham's suspicions about Lord Ruskin, Amy hoped they were caused by nothing more than jealousy. Her aunt seemed convinced that the earl would never cross the line of what was proper, and Amy hoped the lady was correct. It would prove difficult if Mrs. Reed was wrong, for then they must avoid the gentleman, which meant Amy might never have the opportunity to come to know the earl's intriguing cousin, Sir Hartley.

"Do you mean you cannot offer me any assistance?" Sir Hartley put down the tankard of fine ale he'd been enjoying at the Roman Folly Inn and frowned at Henry Baker. The constable was a stocky man in his mid thirties with a plain, honest face and thinning brown hair that he wore long about his shoulders.

"Sir Hartley, 'tis not that I can't help, but what's the purpose? I've done enough investigatin' to know that it ain't one of the servants from either house that's been robbed. I simply don't have enough men to put one in every fashionable establishment in Bath. Besides, sir, you know as well as I that if it turns out to be some gentry swell, he won't never see the inside of the gaol."

Hart's gaze dropped to the pewter tankard, knowing Mr. Baker had the right of it. The best they could hope for was to put a stop to the thieving by threats of public exposure and demand the stolen items be returned. "Then I guess I shall have to enlist the help of friends I can trust who would be able to attend these cursed parties."

The constable pulled a watch from his waistcoat pocket to view the time, then shut the silver piece with a click. "That seems the best course of action to me, sir. I shall inform you at once if I hear of any further thefts. If you come up with a suspect, I can send a couple of lads to tail him and perhaps catch him if he tries to sell his ill-gotten booty."

There was little Sir Hartley could do to protest. He bade the constable farewell, then sat and finished his ale, running the names of his friends through his mind. He tried to think of someone who would be willing to come to Bath and engage in a bit of intrigue. His old Eton friend Lord Montieth was recently married and not likely to abandon his lovely bride. Shamus O'Brien, a Corinthian like himself, had returned to Ireland for several months hoping to find some new filly to debut on the track. Then he thought of Colonel Maxwell Hensley, a friend he hadn't seen in two years. The man had returned to York to mourn the loss of his father, who had died on the hunting field, and to try to bring the estate back from Dun territory. This might be just the thing to entice the former soldier from his self-imposed isolation.

That settled in his mind, Sir Hartley tossed several coins on the table and called for his curricle. He would write at once and send the letter express. With any luck he might have Max in Bath by the end of the week. He climbed into his carriage and set out for Ruskin Terrace.

Still on the outskirts of town and unfettered by traffic, the baronet drove his carriage at a spanking pace. As he took the curve leading toward Vellore Lane, he spied a young lady walking her dog, a servant trailing behind. On closer inspection he realized it was Miss Addington, the very person with whom he'd decided to speak that morning. He didn't know when he'd have another opportunity to warn the lady, so he decided to do so at once.

Amy's gaze settled on the curricle and well-matched bays the moment the rig came into view. At last the carriage drew near enough so she could see that the driver was Sir Hartley Ross, looking every inch the Corinthian in an elegant buff greatcoat over a dark grey morning coat with a grey and white striped waistcoat topping grey buckskins. He reined the carriage to a stylish halt, then rose and sketched something of a bow as he braced one Hessian-clad foot against the splashboard. He held the reins with one hand and tipped his black beaver with the other. A more dashing sight Amy had never seen.

"Good morning, Miss Addington. Have you taken a wrong turn? I can assure you that this road leads out of town. Or did you prefer to take a walk into the countryside?"

"Good day, sir. I have not taken a wrong turn. I am looking for the residence of Captain Jones's widow on this road. A small cottage with a ship's bell in the front garden."

The gentleman grinned, and Amy's heart beat faster. She thought him not the handsomest man she'd ever seen, for her own brother Alexander still held that spot in her mind, but Sir Hartley gave her a decidedly strange sensation in the pit of her stomach.

"I passed such a cottage almost a mile back. Pray allow me to take you up with me and drive you to the lady's front door."

Amy hesitated. She would like nothing better, but decorum told her that it wasn't proper to ride with a gentleman she was scarcely acquainted with, and she knew from her late father's old stories that the rules here in England were rigidly adhered to. Reluctantly she said, "You are too kind, sir, but I would not subject you to young Claudius's dirt in your vehicle."

Sir Hartley eyed the mutt, and his mouth quirked with amusement. "I am quite used to dogs and their dirt, Miss Addington, as are most country gentlemen. In truth, there is a matter about which I should like to speak with you. Your man can jump up behind and the proprieties shall be fulfilled."

Amy's curiosity was piqued. What could this handsome gentleman have to say to her? She signaled Peter to climb onto the back strap, then urged Claudius into the curricle. The dog jumped first to the floor, then continued on to the leather seat, turning around and settling as if he were a veteran traveler. When Amy went to shoo him off, Sir Hartley told her not to do so on his account.

He sat down, looking at the dog, his gaze lingering on first the mangled ear, then the lame foot. "I must tell you, Miss Addington, that your choice of pets tells me a great deal about you."

"And what would that be, sir? That I am a ramshackle

creature with no pretensions to beauty or manners and bark at people with the slightest provocation?"

Sir Hartley's gaze flew to her face; then seeing the twinkling in her doe-brown eyes, he laughed. "Not a bit of it, and well you must know if you have a cheval glass at home. What Claudius tells me about you is that you have a kind heart and little worry about what Society may think."

"Well, I shall have to speak to Claudius about gossiping behind my back. He knows all my darkest secrets." Amy stroked the black dog's chin, and in turn the animal leaned his head against her.

"A lady with dark secrets—how intriguing." The baronet laughed, then neatly turned the carriage around and headed in the direction in which he had come. As they bowled along the nearly empty road, Amy admired the gentleman's skill with the ribbons. She remained quiet, wondering what he wanted to say to her.

Sir Hartley wrestled in his mind with how to tell her what his cousin was planning without completely betraying Silas or offending the young lady. He decided there was nothing for it but to dive right into the heart of the matter. "Miss Addington, I hope you won't think I am overstepping my bounds, but I would give you a word of caution regarding Miss Reed. She is quite the most beautiful young lady I've ever seen, and thus will attract a variety of gentlemen with suspect motives. You must be wary."

Amy's heart plummeted. It seemed that, like Mr. Latham, the baronet was jealous of the attentions others paid to her cousin, and he was as taken with Helen as all the rest who'd met her yesterday. Her hand tightened on Claudius's tether and she stared straight ahead, trying to quell her disappointment.

Unaware of the young lady's reaction as he handled his spirited team, Sir Hartley continued. "I understand that you are newly arrived in England and may not be aware of my cousin's reputation with beautiful women."

The young lady's chin came up defiantly. "On that you are mistaken, sir. I have been informed. But I was led to believe that they were women of a certain type. Do you compare my cousin with such females?"

Hart swore under his breath. He was handling this rather badly. A different tack was called for. "You needn't bark at me," he teased, hoping to lighten the mood, but a glance told him that the young lady wasn't amused. On a more sober note, he continued, "You mistake me, Miss Addington. I believe your cousin to be a genteel young lady. But I also know what is expected of my cousin by his family in the matter of his marriage. He may be enamored with Miss Reed's beautiful face, but I would not wish her to have her hopes raised in regards to an offer of marriage that shall never come. When the time comes, Lord Ruskin will marry a woman of birth and fortune, as is expected of someone of his station."

His words were like a slap in the face. Clearly, the earl and Sir Hartley thought Helen well beneath their touch due to her impoverished circumstances. What must they think of a mere companion? In clipped tones, she said, "I understand you fully, sir."

They rode on in strained silence, Amy incensed and Sir Hartley berating himself for having been too direct. At last the baronet drew the carriage to a halt in front of a neat little stone cottage with clusters of ivy growing in irregular patterns on the wall. A ship's bell, polished to a high gloss, hung on a post beside the gate; beyond lay an unkempt garden. White stepping stones led to a weathered oak door.

Sir Hartley called to the footman to go to the horses' heads, then eyed the house with doubt. "Are you certain there is anyone here, Miss Addington? It looks quite abandoned."

Amy, still annoyed with him, nodded her head and kept her gaze locked on the cottage. "This is where our butler said he purchased the dogs."

Hart jumped down and went to the gate. He knew he'd deeply offended Miss Addington, and that hadn't been his intention. He wanted to do all in his power to put matters to right. He was also curious why she'd returned to the lady who'd supplied the scruffy hound. Was she intending to return the lovable creature? "Shall we see if anyone is home?" With that, he tugged the rope and clanged the bell.

Immediately a clamor of barks sounded inside the small building. Minutes later the door edged open and a veritable sea of ragtag dogs in all shapes and sizes poured into the garden. A small, thin, grey-haired woman dressed in black bombazine covered with a large white apron appeared in the opening. She gazed curiously at her visitors with a pleasant smile, then stepped onto her stoop, wiping her hands on her apron. "Welcome to Crow's Nest Cottage. What may I do for you?"

Before Amy could explain her reason for coming, Mrs. Jones's gaze fell on Claudius and she frowned. "Why, it's my Ernest. Don't tell me he's been giving you trouble, for a sweeter dog there never was. Were you wanting me to take him back, miss?"

"Oh, no, Mrs. Jones. Claudius, as I call him, is a treasure. I came because Bigelow told me what a wonderful thing you are doing here taking care of so many stray animals, and I thought I might help you in some small way."

The lady's grey brows rose in surprise. "I've never turned down a helping hand, child, but who are you?"

"I am Miss Addington." Miffed at the baronet, she decided not to introduce him to the widow.

Mrs. Jones, unaware of the rift between the pair, looked to the gentleman and gave a charming half grin. "I could certainly use a strong back at the moment."

Amy's cheeks flamed pink. Why had she allowed her anger to make her appear rude? It seemed the widow was thinking to use him like a mere servant. "Oh, Mrs. Jones, this is Sir Hartley Ross who was kind enough to drive me here. I have my aunt's footman if you have need of something to be lifted. I do not think—"

"Your man is busy with my horses, Miss Addington." Sir Hartley shoved his hat back a bit, giving him a boyish charm at odds with his age. He grinned at Mrs. Jones. "May I be of assistance to you, madam?"

The captain's widow came forward and opened the gate, inviting her visitors into the cottage. "You must take tea with me, for I am certain you need to warm yourselves after being out in this cold weather."

Sir Hartley followed the ladies into the small front parlor of the house. The room was neat and cozy despite the worn appearance of the overstuffed chintz chairs. "I cannot speak for Miss Addington, but I would welcome a spot of tea, madam. But first I believe you have a task for me?"

Mrs. Jones urged Amy to be seated in front of the fire and led the baronet through a door into the kitchen. All the dogs remained crowding around Amy and Claudius, so she sat down in an armchair near the fire and began to pet the eager noses that came up to sniff the visitor. When the curious dogs at last settled on the floor, she took off her bonnet and sat back to ponder her conversation with the gentleman in the carriage.

As she gazed at the closed door, her thoughts were very disordered. It had been something of a surprise to find Sir Hartley so proud and unbending on matters of marriage. He hadn't seemed so the other day, but clearly he saw himself and his cousin above their touch, no matter them having an uncle who was a baron, but then he didn't know that, did he? Still, his pride made his easy manners and camaraderie with Mrs. Jones all the more puzzling. But then it wasn't as if he were intending on marrying the Widow Jones, now was it?

As the clock on the mantelpiece ticked away the minutes, Amy managed to order her thoughts a bit more. Was it possible that it wasn't a matter of the baronet being overly proud, as she'd rashly concluded? Might he genuinely be trying to warn her that Lord Ruskin was not a man to be trusted with a beautiful young girl? Noel had said the same thing, yet she'd casually dismissed it as jealousy. Uncertain what to think, Amy simply promised herself that she would do her best to discourage Helen from forming a tendre for the handsome young earl.

Some minutes later Sir Hartley returned, brushing bits of dust from his greatcoat before he removed it and casually tossed it over the back of a chair. There was a speculative look in his green eyes as he moved to take a seat opposite Amy's. He appeared uncertain what to expect after their earlier conversation. "Mrs. Jones will be here with the tea in a moment."

"Were you able to help her?"

The gentleman grinned. "The lady had a few sacks of meal for me to move into the storeroom. Her maid is gone to Bristol to see her ailing mother at present." He paused a moment, a contrite expression settling on his features. "While we have this bit of privacy, I should like to apologize. I didn't mean to offend you, Miss Addington. The truth is that I know little of you and your family and in no way meant to disparage you, your cousin or your present circumstances. What I do know is Lord Ruskin, and I have seen ample evidence that around beautiful women he takes leave of his good sense. I shall not betray his confidences, but I will tell you that marriage is not part of his present plans in regards to Miss Reed."

Amy sat stroking a small mottled black terrier that had jumped into her lap while she listened to the gentleman apologize. Her gaze locked with Sir Hartley's, and in that moment she realized that no matter his feelings or lack thereof for Helen, he was genuinely trying to warn her to beware of his cousin. Something dastardly must be afoot in the earl's plans to make his relative so adamant in issuing such a warning, but she wouldn't press him to betray the man's confidence any further. "Then I must thank you for your honesty, sir. I shall do my best to convince Helen to look elsewhere for love."

At that moment Mrs. Jones entered carrying a tray laden with tea and buttered bread. Amy and Sir Hartley had gone a long way to removing the constraint between them, and the three of them had a comfortable half-hour as Mrs. Jones told the tale of how she came to be keeper of so many animals. First there had been an injured mastiff she called George. She had found the great, hulking dog at the garden gate and had nursed the fellow back to health. Then slowly her collection grew to include three stray pugs she'd dubbed Sophia, Elizabeth and Amelia. Then came two injured terriers she'd named William and Edward. Mrs. Jones turned and pointed to four bedraggled-looking foxhounds lying on the rug near the door, saying they were the newest residents. They were called Frederick, Adolphus, Octavius and Augusta.

Sir Hartley laughed. He bent down and picked up a black and white King Charles spaniel. "Let me guess. This is either Mary or Charlotte."

A twinkle came into Mrs. Jones's faded blue eyes. "That is Charlotte. I see you have caught on to my little jest."

Amy looked a question at the pair as they laughed. "How did you know her name, sir?"

Sir Hartley put the dog back on the rug and picked up his cup. "I believe that Mrs. Jones has a fondness for the regent and his siblings."

"Poppycock, my good man." Mrs. Jones gave a mock glare across her own cup at him. " 'Tis my view that the royal family behaves little better than a pack of mongrels with their court scandals, excessive debts and littering the country with their baseborn brats. I have chosen their names to bestow on these little lost creatures to bring a little dignity back to King George's family."

Not having lived in England, Amy knew little of court intrigue or the royals, but she found she liked Mrs. Jones very much. Remembering her reason for coming, she picked up her reticule and reached in for her coin purse. "I should like to give you a little something to help out with the expense of—"

The widow waved the proffered money away. "That won't be necessary, child. Sir Hartley was before you in offering his help when I explained how I collect lost and injured animals. We shall do very nicely with his kind largess."

Amy blinked, then looked at the baronet, who was offering a bit of buttered bread to Charlotte, who sat on her haunches with paws up begging for a bite. There could be no denying that Sir Hartley Ross was an intriguing man. Then she remembered his warning about his cousin and knew that she must do her best to keep Helen away from the gentleman's cousin.

Soon Sir Hartley rose and offered to drive Amy home. They bade farewell to Mrs. Jones, who invited them to come again. Amy promised to try to visit, but she informed the widow that her time was not her own. Outside, the gentleman helped her into his carriage and in minutes they were off for Bath. He kept up a steady stream of polite conversation about Mrs. Jones, the dogs and the weather, but Amy found her spirits low. She'd come to realize that Sir Hartley was the one gentleman she found interesting. Yet due to his cousin's vices, she must not seek his company when he was with Lord Ruskin. And since he was staying with the earl, they were, no doubt, together a great deal.

"You are very quiet, Miss Addington. Are you still angry with me about our earlier conversation? You know I truly meant no offense."

She shook her head. "I know you were telling me the truth about Lord Ruskin, sir. In fact, I am merely tired. It was kind of you to save me the walk back."

Hart glanced at her and suspected there was a great deal more going on behind those lovely brown eyes— eyes that a man could lose himself in. That thought caused him to fix his own on the road ahead. He knew his own mother would be as appalled as Aunt Roslyn were he to become entangled with a penniless companion. Perhaps it was just as well that he had something to concentrate on while in Bath. It would never do for him to pursue Miss Addington after he'd just warned his own cousin away from Miss Reed, albeit for a very different reason.

Four

Amy thanked Sir Hartley for bringing her home, then hurried up to her room, hoping for a few moments to marshal her thoughts. It was unfortunate that the gentleman was so intimately connected with Lord Ruskin. But she would not risk her cousin's happiness by exposing Helen to the earl if his purpose was to offer her *carte blanche,* and Amy strongly suspected that was why the baronet had taken time to warn her. With a sigh, she went to the window and looked out at the garden that hadn't seen a gardener's tools in some time. Life rarely ran smoothly in her experience. She must keep the baronet out of her thoughts, knowing that circumstances were against them.

A knock sounded on the bedroom door, and before Amy could utter a word, Helen burst into the room, eyes glittering with excitement. "We have been invited to Baroness Simmons's musicale this evening in the Royal Crescent. Mother's friend Mrs. Sanford presented us. Her Ladyship sent round invitations as soon as we returned home. Is that not wonderful? Whatever shall I wear? You must come and help me choose."

Amy arched one delicate black brow. "How shall we journey across town after dark? Surely Aunt does not intend to hire three sedan chairs." They had no carriage in Bath, the solicitor, Mr. Ingram, insisting it was an expense they could ill afford.

"Why, your friend Mr. Latham was present and said he would be glad to escort us. Mama accepted his kind offer. How do you think I should wear my hair?" Helen rushed to the mirror, turning her head back and forth to observe her countenance. "Should I go Grecian with lots of curls? Or perhaps a bit plainer for a mere musicale?"

Hardly listening to Helen's chatter, Amy reflected on the generosity of Mr. Latham to offer them transportation. She knew he was enamored with her cousin. Amy glanced thoughtfully to where the girl stood pulling pins from her hair.

"Helen, do you admire Mr. Latham?"

"Oh, he is well enough for a plain mister, but Mama says I must settle for nothing less than an earl and one that still has money." Helen grabbed her cousin's brush and began to untangle her golden tresses.

A heaviness settled in Amy's chest. It was going to be very difficult to steer her ambitious young relative away from Lord Ruskin, for he fit exactly Aunt Vivian's ideal of the perfect husband. There was also the matter of her friend Mr. Latham being hurt. He was a kind young man who appeared to have little chance to win Helen's heart.

Yet Amy would not fall into despair. While she could do little to prevent Noel's broken heart other than to discourage his suit, she would try to wield her influence over the biddable young beauty before her as far as other gentlemen were concerned. Hopefully, she would help Helen come to realize that a gentleman's worth was not his title or money as Aunt Vivian was suggesting, but his character and goodness. She suddenly remembered Sir Hartley's kindness to Mrs. Jones, but she knew she didn't want to recommend that gentleman as a model for fear that Helen would pursue him. No matter her duty to her aunt to help find a husband for her cousin, Amy simply would not encourage the girl to look in that direction. Sir Hartley was far too old for a madcap eighteen-year-old anyway, or so Amy told herself to excuse her decision.

On that thought, she took the brush from Helen. "Here is what I would suggest." She worked with skill, while beginning her plan of attack. "It's very exciting being invited to parties here in Bath, but there is no hurry to attach yourself to a gentleman, my dear. Remember, my sister shall return from Italy this year. Wouldn't you rather wait until then? No doubt she will invite us to London, and everything will likely be of the first stare. I understand that my new brother-in-law is wealthy. Being presented under Lord and Lady Borland's auspices is no small thing. It would certainly discourage any improper behavior."

"I shan't behave improperly," Helen bristled, glaring at her cousin in the mirror.

Amy rolled her eyes heavenward as she swore, *"Santa Clello"* under her breath. Then to her cousin she said, "I didn't mean your improper behavior. I was referring to rogues who think they can take advantage of young ladies who don't have male family members to protect their good name. What you must remember is you are very young and have plenty of time to fall in love."

Helen reached up to pat a curl at her ear into place. "I should adore attending all the fashionable balls in London." She paused and bit at her lip thoughtfully before adding, "But I shan't whistle down any offers while we are here. After all, if I bring Lord Ruskin up to scratch, he is wealthy enough to take me to London."

Clearly it was going to be a hard-fought battle to keep such a willing victim from the earl's clutches. Amy's only hope was that now that she was forewarned, she had a distinct advantage over the gentleman. And for that she owed Sir Hartley a debt of thanks which she doubted she could ever repay.

The remainder of the day was filled with plans for the evening's entertainment. Amy welcomed the distraction. It helped to temper her own disappointment in having to avoid the baronet. By eight that evening the ladies were dressed and awaiting Mr. Latham's carriage.

Helen sailed into the drawing room, a vision in pink crepe de chine over a white satin underskirt. Pink and white satin roses had been worked into her blonde curls. Her aqua eyes were shining with excitement, making her more beautiful than ever. Amy wore one of the new gowns she'd fashioned from the material purchased during the Basingstoke shopping trip. The dress was a blue glacé silk with white Bruges lace at the collar and sleeves. She'd thought herself very fine until she saw Helen in all her blonde glory.

Mrs. Reed, in dark grey Florence satin with a matching turban, was well pleased with her daughter and even acknowledged that Amy, too, was splendid. "This is an important affair, girls, so you must mind your manners and do nothing to give anyone a disgust of you."

Helen, standing watch at the window, cried, "Mr. Latham's carriage is here."

The gentleman was soon ushered into the parlor, and he complimented the ladies profusely, but he could scarcely take his eyes off Helen. For her part, the young beauty paid scant notice to the young man's feelings; instead she rushed past him in her eagerness to go. In the carriage she chattered about who would be attending the affair.

Mrs. Reed, eyeing young Latham, appeared vastly pleased that her daughter had made so easy a conquest despite his being a mere mister. She sat like a cat who'd finished off the cream pot, smiling all the way to the musicale. Amy could only wish that some miracle would occur that would open her cousin's eyes to Noel Latham's excellent qualities. He was worth ten of the Earl of Ruskin in character. But she owned too much of the Addington practicality to pin her hopes on a supernatural event changing her cousin's thinking.

As the carriage entered the Royal Crescent, Amy wondered if Sir Hartley would be present. She shook her head as if to rid it of the thought. If the gentleman were there, that would likely mean the earl would be, too. She gave a soft sigh. She didn't want to have to spend the entire evening trying to keep Helen away from a hardened rake.

"What the devil are you staring at so intently?" Lord Ruskin came to stand beside his cousin, who stood at the top of Lady Simmons's staircase watching the crush of people arrive in the marble foyer below.

"Merely the arriving guests. Thought I recognized an old friend, but I was mistaken," Hart prevaricated. His true reason for being there was to see if any of the night's guests might be a candidate for thievery—some lord known to be under the hatches, or perhaps a younger son on an allowance with a taste for games of chance. Truth be told, there were so many of that ilk littering the *ton* at any given party, he didn't know where to begin.

"Come," Ruskin urged. "Mother insists you meet some of her intimate friends."

This part of Hart's visit to Bath was a rather inconvenient necessity. He needed to be included in his aunt's invitations, therefore he must make his bows to all the hostesses. With a certain reluctance he followed Silas into the music room, which had been readied for the concert featuring Signora Violetta Navarro, the most sought-after sensation to arrive on the shores of England since Catalani and Naldi.

Hart greeted several gentlemen he recognized as he followed his cousin through the open double doors. Inside, neat rows of chairs arched in a half circle around a pianoforte in front of the chamber. A small string quartet plucked at their instruments while awaiting the diva.

Silas slowed his pace and lowered his voice. "Best be warned Mother is in one of her matchmaking moods. Cannot stand to see a fellow single and happy."

Hart's gaze moved to where his aunt stood with a cluster of females about her. He nearly groaned at the notion that Aunt Roslyn might be trying to include him in her marriage schemes. Was it not enough that he had his own mother plotting toward the same ends when he was in London? He'd hoped for a respite while in Bath, but it appeared that was not to be.

The countess, in conversation with a rather formidable-looking lady, caught sight of the approaching gentlemen. "Ah, there you are, Hart." His aunt took his arm in a viselike grip, then turned to the gathered females. "Lady Munsford, Lady Cecilia Murray, Miss Murray and Miss Walker, allow me to present my nephew, Sir Hartley Ross. Dear boy, this is the marchioness, her daughter and nieces come to Bath for a bit of entertainment during the winter."

Lady Munsford lifted her lorgnette, bowing her head slightly with condescension. She was a tall woman who'd clearly been a beauty in her youth. But time, or perhaps the infamous womanizing of the marquess, had taken its toll on her features. There were but brief glimpses of her former self when the lady's mouth relaxed from its grim set. At present, she appeared a rather overpowering female in deep red silk who saw little to interest her in a mere baronet. Hart breathed a relieved sigh.

Beside her mother, Lady Cecilia unbent enough to offer Sir Hartley two fingers, garnering a frown from Lady Munsford. The daughter equaled her mother in height, but where the marchioness was ample, Lady Cecilia stood rail thin. Her dress of ecru satin with a gauze overskirt appeared cleverly designed to disguise her feminine shortcomings with rows of blond lace trimming the bodice. The young lady's one true claim to beauty was her shining brown hair, which hung in abundant curls from a small gold filigree headdress fashioned like a crown.

The third female, Miss Murray, stood in silence a step behind her cousin, never opening her mouth. She was a mouse of a girl with pale brown hair scraped away from a thin face and bound tightly at her neck. The marchioness had left little to chance that one might find the girl anything but a companion by dressing her in a drab grey silk gown without trim.

The final lady, Miss Walker, gave Hart a bit more to worry about. She was a petite redhead attired in a gown with more ruffles and bows than was the current fashion. She dimpled at Hart, then thrust her hand at him so that he had little choice but to kiss the gloved surface. He reluctantly obliged, then stepped back, feeling uncomfortable as she continued to eye him as if he were a sweetmeat she were about to devour. "Do you stay long in Bath, Sir Hartley?"

"A few weeks only, Miss Walker."

The young lady opened her mouth as if to again speak, but thankfully Lady Munsford caught her eye. She frowned, and so Miss Walker sighed and fell silent, but never removed her gaze from the baronet.

As a brief silence fell over the group, the marchioness took the lead in the conversation. "Well, Sir Hartley, you will do well enough to entertain my nieces for an evening."

The lady sounded as if she were bestowing a privilege on him. Hart politely sketched a slight bow and wondered how he might escape from such a duty. He had important business to attend and hadn't the time to be dancing attendance on two young ladies.

With that detail taken care of, Lady Munsford turned and began interrogating Silas on his stay in Bath. A rather sullen expression settled on the earl's handsome features as he struggled to remain civil while the lady pried into his activities.

Silas shot his cousin a look of frustration. At last, in desperation the earl engaged Lady Cecilia in conversation about life in Cumberland, which was the Marquess of Munsford's family seat. The young lady appeared only a bit more animated as she spoke of her home, but even that did little to improve her cheerless looks.

As Hart watched his cousin struggle to converse with the nearly mute Lady Cecilia, it flashed through his mind that his aunt had taken leave of her senses to think her son would consider such an ordinary female for a wife. Silas was a connoisseur of beauty. One certainly expected such a man to marry a diamond of the first water. Not this shy, unprepossessing girl, no matter her fortune and birth.

Remembering his own manners, Sir Hartley made an effort to make small talk with the other young ladies. He started with Miss Murray, but received only several monosyllabic responses to his inquiry as to how she liked Bath. Miss Walker was more than delighted to fill the gap. She chattered for several minutes about the sights she'd seen, then about her coming Season in London.

"I do adore parties. Do you attend all the functions

in Town during the Season, sir? Tell me what I might expect."

"Mostly boredom." Seeing the disappointment on the young lady's face, Hart felt guilty and amended his statement. "Pardon my cynicism, but I fear I am well past being interested in the social whirl of London, Miss Walker. I try to avoid such affairs like the plague. You must inquire of such matters from my cousin. I believe he enjoys such affairs."

Miss Walker cast a covert glance at the earl, but Lady Munsford had warned her nieces away from Lady Cecilia's suitor. Turning her grey eyes back on the baronet, the redhead tried another tack. "Lady Ruskin tells us you are a famous whip, Sir Hartley." She coyly fluttered her lashes at him.

It took all Hart could do not to laugh at the young lady's silly attempt at flirting. "No more so than the average gentleman, Miss Walker. I would say I have managed to master the art of driving." He suddenly wondered where that cursed singer was.

"Back in Cumberland, I tool my own carriage everywhere. A neat little curricle with a perfectly matched set of greys. Unfortunately, Aunt Munsford won't allow me to drive in Bath. She thinks it unladylike. If only I had someone who might take me driving and would allow me to handle his ribbons." She looked expectantly at the gentleman.

"Very few people drive in Bath, Miss Walker. The hills, you know," Hart replied noncommittally. From his position in the group he faced the door of the music room. His gaze locked on an acquaintance who entered the room, and he announced, "Oh, there is Lord Marsden. I have been looking all over town for him so I may convey a message from his sister."

Manners prevented him from stranding the young ladies who'd been foisted upon him, so Hart reached out and nabbed a gentleman nearby with whom he had little more than a nodding acquaintance. "Mr. Curtis, allow me to present Miss Walker and Miss Murray. Curtis here is a devil with the ribbons, Miss Walker." The baronet meant that literally, but the young man took it as a compliment and smiled with pride. "Ladies, may I introduce you to Viscount Barton's nephew. Forgive me for abandoning you, but I promised to give Marsden a very important message."

He felt a veritable coward for deserting his cousin, but he'd seen Miss Walker's type too many times in London. They had a talent for attaching themselves to a gentleman, and before the man knew what had occurred, he was engaged, and very often to protect the chit's name.

Crossing the room, Sir Hartley exchanged pleasantries with Lord Marsden, informing him that his sister was lamenting not having seen him in months. The young lord rolled his eyes, saying he couldn't tolerate his sister's houseful of brats, and if fate were kind, it would hopefully be months before she did see him again. The two friends fell into conversation, and Hart remained steadfastly at the rear of the oversized chamber. As the music room filled, the gentlemen shifted their position to the far wall, but Hart made certain he moved no closer to his matchmaking aunt or Miss Walker.

Several other friends came and joined him. When the conversation moved to the current crop of actresses, Hart's thoughts wondered to his mission. Scanning the room, he realized there was nothing of value left to take; everything but chairs and some family portraits had been removed for the concert. Should he politely excuse himself and rove about to find a room with a selection of easily transportable items? Looking around, he realized the seats were rapidly filling and the singer would soon begin.

At that moment Miss Addington stepped through the open double doors, and Sir Hartley's gaze roved over her trim figure. She was a vision in blue silk, her raven locks fashioned in a riot of curls atop her head with a star-burst gold clasp. He knew a sudden urge to go and greet her, and then his reason returned. If Miss Addington was in attendance, then so was her cousin.

Minutes later Miss Reed entered the music room on Mr. Latham's arm. An angular, raw-boned woman trailed behind the pair that one would never think was the beauty's mother because of her plainness, yet Hart suspected the lady was, as she fussed with the young lady's ribbons and shawl. Nearly every masculine head in the place swiveled in the girl's direction. There was no denying the chit was ravishing. He glanced to where his cousin remained trapped with Lady Cecilia, and even from this distance Hart could see the raw lust in the man's eyes as they settled on Miss Reed. His stomach clenched with disgust for the earl. Something more would have to be done to turn Silas from his plans to seduce the girl.

Fortunately, just as Ruskin started to take his leave of Lady Cecilia, his mother laid a hand upon his arm. He appeared as if he wanted to protest, but habits won the day, and he did as his mother desired. He led the young lady to one of the green damask gilt chairs, then settled beside her. But Lady Ruskin's victory was only partial, for her son continually glanced over the girl's shoulder to the blonde goddess whose party selected seats near the rear.

Since there were more guests than seats, Hart gladly remained standing in the rear to enjoy the concert with the other gentlemen who lined the back wall. Again he knew an urge to seek out Miss Addington and issue her a second warning to keep her beautiful cousin away from Silas. Then he realized it was a mere excuse to be close enough to gaze into the raven-haired beauty's warm brown eyes.

He must remain focused on his purpose for coming to Bath. With that in mind, he positioned himself near the door so that he might slip out unnoticed and lie in wait for the thief, should the villain choose to strike.

Seated at the end of the last row of chairs, Amy covertly watched Sir Hartley and his friends converse at the back of the room as Signora Navarro took her place near the pianoforte. The singer was greeted with a smattering of applause. The baronet looked handsome in his black evening coat over a white waistcoat. Her aunt drew Amy's attention away from the gentleman when she grasped her niece's arm.

Mrs. Reed's eager gaze swept the crowd. She asked, in a whispered undertone, "Is Lord Ruskin in attendance? I should like to see him for myself."

Amy leaned closer to her too-ambitious relation. "I am hearing dreadful things about the gentleman, Aunt. Pray don't encourage Helen to pursue him. I don't think that even her beauty would bring him up to scratch. Even his cousin tells me that the earl might act the scoundrel with a gently bred girl."

Vivian Reed's eyes narrowed and her neck arched arrogantly as she glared at Amy. She looked every inch the aristocrat. "We are not without protection, child. All we need do is inform the gentleman that her uncle, Baron Landry, might take exception, and that should put an end to any such foolish notion."

Amy grew desperate to convince her aunt. "But did you not tell me you hadn't spoken with the baron for nearly twenty-five years, ever since Father and Mother were wed in Florence, and your brother cut the connection?" It was a well-known fact that her parents' marriage had created a large chasm in the Addington family that even now existed, and her aunt had sided with her younger brother, Amy's father.

"Well, the earl won't know that, silly girl." Aunt Vivian's voice rose as if she were speaking to a simple child.

"Shush!" A turbaned dowager glared over her shoulder at Mrs. Reed.

With that, the two women fell silent. Amy's gaze moved to the object of their dispute, Lord Ruskin. At that exact moment he glanced back at Helen, and Amy heard her cousin titter as the pair's eyes met. If only Alexander were back from the Continent. The earl would never dare to attempt to entice a young lady into an unseemly alliance with a soldier at her side.

The signora owned a wonderful voice, but Amy found herself distracted. Her gaze roved to the rear of the room, but Sir Hartley was nowhere to be seen. She wondered where he had gotten to, but knowing it was none of her concern, she tried to pay attention to the singer.

Yet Amy found she couldn't concentrate. Her thoughts were filled with turmoil. She needed some argument that would convince her aunt not to pin her hopes on Ruskin. Yet some thirty minutes later, Amy still hadn't a clue what she could say that would make the determined lady heed the warning.

By the time Signora Navarro started her fourth aria, Amy's head had begun to hurt from all her grappling with what seemed an unsolvable dilemma. Never one prone to illness, she was convinced she only needed a bit of fresh air to clear her thoughts. She whispered to her aunt that she was going to step out into the hall for a moment. The passageway stood empty except for a liveried servant who stepped forward to inquire what the young lady needed.

"I have come in search of a bit of fresh air. I fear there are too many people in there for me."

"Very good, miss. May I suggest the Blue Drawing Room? There is a balcony in there." He stepped to open a door down the hall.

Amy, grateful for a few moments alone, moved past the servant into the room. As the door closed behind her, she checked at the sight that greeted her. There in front of a mahogany console table stood Sir Hartley Ross. He appeared to be examining a small gold figurine, one of several depicting classical figures of Greek mythology set in a semicircle on the table. Looking up, he hurriedly set the piece down. "Ah, Miss Addington. A delight to meet you again so soon."

But his tone sounded anything but delighted. Still, Amy found that her heart seemed to skip a beat at the sight of the handsome gentleman. With an effort, she reminded herself that she must not be a fool. "Do you not like the music, sir?"

Hart, embarrassed to be caught snooping, grabbed at the topic, hoping to distract the young lady from finding him here alone, handling Lord Simmons's valuable property. "Perhaps it is the fact that my Italian is so lacking that I am quite lost. I do believe if she were singing a simple English ballad, I would have stayed to listen."

"I should be delighted to interpret the words of the song for you, sir."

Glad that she didn't question why he was alone in the hostess's drawing room, Hart eagerly accepted her offer. "I would be honored if you would do such a favor. I am certain that with your help I might enjoy the music more." He came to where she stood and offered her his arm.

The young lady hesitated a moment, biting at her

lower lip. "Would you do me a favor in turn, Sir Hartley?"

"Gladly, Miss Addington." He was amazed at the way the candlelight reflected hints of blue in her raven curls, making him long to touch their silky softness.

"I have given a great deal of thought about the warning you gave me during the drive back from Mrs. Jones's. Would you make certain that your cousin knows that Miss Reed is not without protection from her relatives?" Her doe-brown eyes gazed at him with earnestness.

Every instinct told him his loyalty should be to his cousin. After all, at the moment there was nothing more than talk from Silas. Like most fashionable young men, the earl had a short attention span, and something else might soon distract him. Hart would like to think the earl wouldn't actually do anything dishonorable. But something about this woman made him want to take his cousin to task for merely having such improper thoughts. "And would there be a name I might give Silas to convince him of the truth of what I say?"

"Our uncle is Baron Landry of Norfolk County."

"Landry! Miss Addington, are you acquainted with the gentleman?"

"N-no. As you know I have only just recently come to England. Is there some problem?"

"My cousin, like most of the *ton*, would have no fear of the baron. Unless Miss Reed were at the bottom of a tankard of ale, Lord Landry couldn't find her with a six-man search party. Lost his fortune on the tables at White's some years ago and has been drowning his sorrows ever since. Truth to tell, he may be in debt, for he frequents some rather low gaming hells in Town. I doubt the man could defend his own honor, let alone that of a young lady."

Amy knew a sudden twinge of regret for her brother who would eventually inherit the barony since Lord

Landry had no sons. Clearly, there would be little left when that occurred. But that was not the point at the moment.

"Then you may inform Lord Ruskin there is my brother, Major Alexander Addington. We expect him to return from France any day." Amy knew that was stretching the truth about Alex's return, yet no worse than using her estranged uncle's name, but at the moment she was desperate.

The gentleman nodded his head as if approving her choice of protectors, then lifted her hand to his arm. "I shall tell him as soon as I may. Shall we return to enjoy our evening and put thoughts of Miss Reed and Lord Ruskin aside for the moment?"

Amy's fingers pressed against the muscular arm of Sir Hartley, and all thoughts of Lord Ruskin, Helen or her brother seemed to fly from her mind. She allowed the gentleman to lead her back toward the music room, but to her disappointment the musicale appeared to be over and the guests poured out the double door toward the stairs in search of refreshments in the dining room below.

The crowd parted as they approached the music room doors and a very annoyed Lady Ruskin, spying her nephew, marched up to Sir Hartley. "Well, Hart, I am very displeased with you and Silas, but that is matter to be discussed later." Her gaze swept over Amy, leaving the young lady in little doubt of the countess's opinion; then she once again glared at her nephew. "Find my son at once and have him escort me home. I have the headache and cannot stay a moment longer."

Surprised at the countess's abruptness, the baronet said, "Aunt, allow me to present Miss Addington."

Her Ladyship gave the slightest of nods. "Forgive me, Miss Addington, but I must leave as soon as possible."

Sir Hartley hesitated, not wanting to leave the young

lady unaccompanied, but Amy gestured toward the music room. "Pray help your aunt, sir. I see mine conversing with her friends."

She watched as the gentleman led his complaining relative down the stairs. Clearly, the lady was upset about something. Wondering what it was all about, Amy made her way through the milling crowd to where her aunt stood in conversation with Mrs. Sanford, a handsome elderly woman dressed in a fashionable lilac silk gown. Helen was nowhere in sight.

"Where is my cousin, Aunt?" Amy asked with some urgency, knowing that Lord Ruskin appeared to be missing as well.

"Why, Mr. Latham took her and Miss Sanford down for refreshment."

Relieved to know that Helen was well watched, Amy allowed her aunt to detain her while Mrs. Sanford questioned her about how she was enjoying Bath. At last, the ladies decided to go to the dining room and partake of the offered refreshments.

On entering the large chamber, Amy's heart sank as she spied Noel standing beside Miss Sanford, a tall girl with dusty curls and a strong resemblance to Mrs. Sanford. They were at the end of one table. Noel held two glasses of champagne while scanning the room, a disgruntled expression on his round face. Amy excused herself from her aunt and her friend who'd stopped to fill plates and hurried to Noel and Miss Sanford.

"Where is Helen?"

"She disappeared after she sent me for a glass of champagne. I hoped she'd gone back to her mother, but I can only guess where she has gotten to. She's been making calf eyes at Ruskin all night. Miss Addington, you *must* warn her about the man, for she only takes my concerns as mere jealousy."

Miss Sanford's brows rose at Mr. Latham's vehemence. "I don't think she is with the earl. She wandered out the door after you left while I was speaking with Lord Simmons. She appeared to be admiring the paintings before she disappeared down the hall."

Amy had no time to stay and tell Noel that her warnings had fallen on deaf ears as well. "I will find her." She hurried out of the dining room and began a room-by-room search as unobtrusively as possible. Within minutes she ran the girl to ground in a small, dimly lit rear parlor in the company of His Lordship. Dismay raced through her at the struck expression on Helen's beautiful face, which seemed to be only inches from Lord Ruskin's. Why, it looked as if the cad had kissed her.

"Lord Ruskin!" Amy practically shouted the man's name in anger. Helen jumped back at the sound of her cousin's voice. "I believe Sir Hartley is searching for you, my lord. Your mother has taken ill and wishes to leave at once."

A slow, beguiling smile settled on the earl's face as he took Helen's hand, and his gaze never left her awestruck face. "I fear I must bid you adieu, fair one. I hope to have the pleasure of seeing you in Sydney Gardens tomorrow." He placed a kiss on the young lady's hand.

The door to the room opened and Sir Hartley stepped in at that moment. His gaze swept the room taking in the situation, before his green eyes locked with Amy's briefly. "Silas, we must go at once. Your mother awaits us in the carriage."

"I am coming." The earl crossed the room without a word to Amy and departed.

The baronet lingered a moment. "Don't lose heart, Miss Addington. I shall tell him about Major Addington at once." With a polite bow, the gentleman departed.

Amy found little comfort in the gentleman's words.

Her cousin had behaved little better than a common baggage. The door had scarcely closed before Amy's pent-up worries caused her to explode. "What can you be thinking to closet yourself with a known rake? Do you wish to be shunned by all of Society?"

Helen, still dazed from her encounter, scarcely seemed to heed her cousin. "I think the earl has fallen in love with me."

Amy wanted to shake her cousin out of her foolish fantasy. "Love—I doubt the man would know the meaning of the word even after he looked it up in a dictionary, Helen. He is accomplished at seducing women. Don't be a complete ninny and fall victim to his smooth words."

"Ninny!" The taunt seemed to penetrate Helen's stupor and fire her anger. She knew she wasn't the most accomplished of females, but she was no dunce either and the word struck a chord. Her days at school had been marred by the other girls calling her names out of jealousy, and she wouldn't tolerate it from her cousin. "Gentlemen do not send flowers to ninnies, Cousin, but then you wouldn't know that, having never received any but from old friends." Tears welled up in her beautiful aqua eyes.

All Amy's anger fled at the sight of her cousin's tears, leaving her feeling like a beast. "Oh, Helen, I didn't mean to insult you, only to gain your attention." She moved across the room and took her cousin's hands. "You must listen to me about Lord Ruskin. Sir Hartley is certain the earl does not intend to offer for you. That he is only trifling with you or worse."

Angered, Helen pulled free and brushed at her tears. "Well, a lot you know about matters of the heart. Has it not occurred to you that Sir Hartley is jealous of his cousin? Remember, I have paid him no particular attention; therefore he says unkind things about Lord Ruskin to ruin our romance."

It would be fruitless to remind Helen that, in fact, the baronet had shown little interest in her. Instead Amy attempted to end their quarrel. "I admit I know nothing of gentlemen, dear Cousin. No doubt you are correct in your assumptions about Sir Hartley. But of one thing I'm certain. Being closeted alone with any gentleman is not done. You don't want to acquire a reputation for being fast here in Bath. It would be the end to your hopes of a grand alliance faster than anything else."

Helen had the decency to blush. "I hadn't intended such a thing to happen. I swear it, Amy. I ran into the gentleman in the hall while I was admiring the paintings, and he asked only for a few moments of my time. We were walking down the passageway for a bit of privacy, and before I knew it we were here and . . . he . . ." Her blush grew deeper and confirmed Amy's suspicion that her cousin had been kissed. Amy was woman enough to wonder what that was like. Seeing the bedazzled expression on Helen's face, there could be little doubt the girl had enjoyed it immensely, which only added to the problem.

"My dear, it only takes one time alone with a gentleman to be discovered and ruined. Society is very unforgiving to young ladies."

Helen tried to look repentant, but her expression owned a remarkable resemblance to a pout. "Well, I shall try not to let it happen again. I promise." Then, seeing the look on Amy's face, she added, "But he is quite the most handsome man I have ever met, and there is his title and money."

Amy sighed with frustration. Helen was so smitten with the idea of being a rich countess that her good sense flew out the window when Ruskin so much as looked her way. Unfortunately, the earl was moving fast to secure her interest, or so it seemed to Amy. If she wasn't vigilant, Helen's effort to land a wealthy, titled husband would be over before it had barely begun.

Still, Amy was determined to do her best to reach her cousin. "I only ask that you remember the proprieties at all times, and I shall be at your side to help. Shall we go find our party? They must be quite ready to leave by now."

Amy put her arm about her cousin and led her back to the hall, but she knew she had set herself a large task. She alone, for there was no depending on Aunt Vivian where Ruskin was concerned, might not be enough, especially against the kisses of an accomplished rake. As they stepped into the dining room, Amy caught sight of Mr. Latham still holding the glasses of champagne. The thought occurred that perhaps she should enlist his help in keeping Helen safe. Truth be told, he was already smitten with the girl. He might as well see her conduct firsthand to open his eyes to her faults and maybe even spare himself further disappointment later on.

On rejoining their party, Amy could see the unmistakable hurt in Mr. Latham's eyes as he handed Helen her drink. A story was quickly fabricated about a torn flounce, but the young man was no fool. It took a great deal of effort by the kind Miss Sanford and Amy to keep the conversation going. But by the time everyone was ready to depart, both Helen and Noel were in better moods and politely discussing Signora Navarro's performance.

Upon returning home, the ladies invited the gentleman in for tea, but he declined due to lateness of the hour. Amy lingered at the door a moment longer than her aunt and cousin. "Would you do me the honor of calling on me early in the morning, Mr. Latham? It would prove a great service to my cousin."

Noel's gaze followed Helen as she disappeared up the stairs. "I would do anything for Miss Reed." Then as an afterthought he smiled politely, adding, "Or for you, Miss Addington."

The time was set for ten, and Amy bade her friend good night. As Bigelow closed the door, she recalled the promise Sir Hartley had made before he departed. She hoped the threat of Alexander and his supposed arrival would keep the earl from continuing with his plans for Helen.

Amy sighed. Between them, she and Sir Hartley might yet keep each of their cousins safe from each other. If only their meetings could be about more pleasant matters, but fate seemed to be against them. On that melancholy thought, she hurried to catch her aunt before the lady retired for the evening, hoping to convince her that Lord Ruskin's interest was not for the right reasons.

The door to Lord Ruskin's carriage had barely closed against the chilled night air before Lady Ruskin voiced her displeasure with both her son and nephew. "I seem to be blessed with two of the most ungrateful relations in all of England. Monstrously ungrateful."

"Monstrously ungrateful?" Lord Ruskin repeated.

Her Ladyship glared at her son. "I have worked for weeks to procure Lady Munsford's good opinion of you so you might pay addresses to her daughter, and you have ruined it all in a single night. Fifty thousand pounds tossed aside so that you could gawk at some vulgar little blonde nobody."

"Vulgar!" Silas parroted, a hint of belligerence in his tone.

"Stop repeating what I say. You sound like some village lackwit."

"But Miss Reed is a diamond of the first water, Mother."

"Diamond! Penniless females can never be called that, dear boy. A paste copy at best."

Silas slumped down in the seat, looking like a recalcitrant five-year-old from his mother's browbeating. "Well, I never asked you to find me a bride, Mother. Besides I wouldn't want that tallow-faced chit across the breakfast table from me for a lifetime for twice the sum of her dowry."

Receiving no satisfaction from her son, she vented her spleen on her nephew. "And you, Hart, running off from Miss Walker after receiving Lady Munsford's blessing. What can you have been about? I know you are quite wealthy, but how could you turn your nose up at a young lady with twenty thousand pounds? One can never have too much money. And don't think I don't know that that little raven-haired wench is related to Silas's little upstart. I have friends in Bath who keep me informed. They are barely respectable, living out in some outlandish place on the outskirts of town. Merely hangers-on in good Society."

"Aunt Roslyn, as I often advise my mother, I am perfectly capable of finding my own wife when the time comes. As to Miss Reed and Miss Addington, while it is true there is little money there, the blood is good. They are in fact the nieces of Baron Landry."

A look of horror settled on Lady Ruskin's face. "Landry! That drunken old gamester whose town house was sold at auction last year? Why, that is even worse than being a nobody. I demand you stay away from that creature, Silas."

"I have no intention of offering matrimony to the likes of Miss Reed . . . or any other female at present, Mother," the earl snapped, a sulky look on his handsome features.

Hart sat amazed at the way his aunt seemed to hold such sway over her grown son. As he'd predicted, she disliked the penniless Miss Reed extremely. It suddenly occurred to him that his aunt was his best ally in this situation. Besides, this was an opportunity to fulfill his promise to Miss Addington. "Perhaps you had best stay clear of the young lady so as not to give rise to expectations of Mrs. Reed and Society at large. I understand the young lady's cousin Major Addington is due in Bath any day. He might take exception to you trifling with his cousin, and, like most soldiers, I would guess him to be a deadly shot."

In the dim light of the carriage, Hart couldn't determine his cousin's reaction to the information since Silas made no comment, but the countess screeched about duels and fell into a fit of the vapors. While he regretted involving his aunt, Hart hoped that he had at last succeeded in putting an end to his cousin's plans.

It took both men to assist the lady into the house at Laura Place. Only after promises that Hart would see that no harm came to her son did Lady Ruskin at last retire for the evening. As the two men departed the lady's sitting room, Silas reach out and grabbed Hart's arm.

"That was a cursed scaley thing to do. My liaisons are none of my mother's affair."

Hart experienced only the slightest twinge of guilt for having involved the countess. At least she might be able to exert some control over her son. "You seem to think that your conduct won't affect Aunt Roslyn in the least, but you cannot create the kind of scandal you are contemplating and not have Bath hold her in part responsible."

Silas sneered, "You've grown old and staid before your time, old man. Even Mother thinks Miss Reed a veritable nobody. I think Bath Society would take little note if the young lady permanently disappeared from the scene."

Hart arched one brow. "Be careful of the game you play, Cousin. You might find that Mrs. Reed won't allow her daughter to be set up as your mistress without shouting to the rooftops. Don't forget Major Addington as well."

"Bah! I never knew a penniless soldier that wouldn't sell his own soul for the right price." The earl smugly grinned. "England really should pay the poor devils more for risking their lives for home and hearth." He then turned and strolled down the stairs.

Hart stared after his cousin, a rising dislike of the young man growing deep within him. But he knew that Silas wasn't that different from most of the titled young men in Society. Money and power allowed them to care little about the less fortunate.

He slowly made his way to his own room, worn down by frustration at both situations he faced. As his waiting valet removed his coat, he clung to the hope that his aunt might yet put a stop to Silas's plot. A nagging mother often proved more useful than Society's disapproval. If Miss Reed were fortunate, she'd seen the last of Ruskin this evening. Yet there remained in Hart the hope that one day he might again meet Miss Addington once her beautiful but flighty cousin was safely married and he was done with catching this thief in Bath.

Five

Noel Latham arrived at Mrs. Reed's home the following morning at ten sharp. To Amy's dismay, he was accompanied by his friend Lord Malcolm. It precluded her from informing the gentleman about Lord Ruskin's conduct the previous evening and seeking his help in protecting Helen.

Upon being ushered into the small, cluttered rear parlor, the gentlemen were all agog with the latest *on-dit* as Claudius sniffed cautiously at their boots. At last satisfied that no danger loomed for his mistress, the dog settled on the rug in front of the fireplace.

"Have you heard the news, Miss Addington?" The thin young lord was positively gleeful as he took a seat. " 'Tis all over Bath this morning that Lady Simmons was robbed during the musicale last night. I was there only briefly, but because it was a dreadful crush I left and went round to see a friend who recently purchased a set of dappled grey Arabs that are touted to be able to take over an hour off the drive from London to Bath."

Ignoring the young man's fixation on horses, Amy asked, "Where did you hear there was a robbery?" She couldn't believe such a story. While robberies had been fairly common in the shabbier parts of Rome where her family had lived, she'd never expected to hear about such things in Bath.

"At the Pump Room when we dropped my mother off. It was the talk of all the old tabbies who come supposedly for the waters, but everyone knows they live for the latest gossip."

"Gossip? Are you certain the story is true?" Amy smiled at the young lord as if to say one must doubt such uncertain tales.

"My mother's friend Mrs. Barkley had it from Lord Simmons himself this very morning."

"Then there can be little doubt the tale is true. I am very sorry for the baroness, for she must be terrified to think of a housebreaker creeping about her home in the night. I feel certain I would never again feel safe in my house had someone broken in and robbed me while I was asleep."

"But it wasn't a housebreaker, Miss Addington. The piece was taken at the musicale." Lord Malcolm nodded his head about such an alarming fact as he noted the shock on the young lady's face. "Lady Simmons saw the piece the afternoon of her party, even discussed putting it and several companion pieces away with one of the servants. Then after all the guests departed, she realized it was missing and summoned her staff. There is no question it was on the table at the beginning of the evening and gone at the end."

It seemed impossible to Amy that someone of Bath's most elite company could have stolen from their hostess. But then she realized she was new to the ways of English Society. "It must have been something very small for anyone to have gotten it out of the house without being seen. Did you hear what exactly was stolen?"

"Just some little gold knickknack from one of the drawing rooms is all I heard. Small, but valuable."

Amy's stomach plummeted. The memory of seeing Sir Hartley holding just such an article in Her Ladyship's drawing room came to her mind. Then she reminded herself that the gentleman had returned the statue to the table—but had he already placed another in his pocket before she'd arrived? Her mind went numb at the thought.

Bigelow entered the room at that moment, giving Amy a moment to recover from her shock. She had no proof the baronet had stolen anything, but what should she do? Her mind was numb at the possibility that a man she admired might be a thief. There could be no doubt that she owed Sir Hartley a debt for having warned her of Lord Ruskin. But she couldn't sit idly knowing Sir Hartley might be stealing from his friends.

"Miss Addington?"

Startled from her musing, Amy found Mr. Latham looking at her, a puzzled expression on his face. "I apologize, sir. I fear you caught me woolgathering over such shocking news as having a thief among our acquaintances."

"You needn't worry that it's anyone you know." Her friend smiled reassuringly. "Doubtless it will turn out to be some hardened gamester trying to keep the bill collectors at bay. Truth be told, it happens more often than we would like to think, but mostly is kept quiet to avoid scandal."

"No doubt you are correct, sir." Amy smiled wanly, sick with her notion of who it might have been. Could Sir Hartley be in financial trouble?

"Now, Miss Addington, you had a request of me?" Mr. Latham and Lord Malcolm eyed her expectantly.

A knock sounded on the door, saving Amy from having to fabricate some tale, for she had no intention of involving Lord Malcolm in the confidential matters of her cousin. This business was too delicate a situation since it involved an earl.

Helen stepped into the room dressed in her pink

walking dress and matching bonnet. "Oh, I didn't know you had guests, Cousin."

Amy knew at once where her young relative was going. "I think we should not walk in Sydney Gardens today." She tried to catch the girl's eye to remind her of the discussion they'd had the previous evening, but Helen was fluttering her lashes at Lord Malcolm.

Then Amy's words penetrated the young lady's antics and her chin rose defiantly. She glared at her cousin. "Mama said we must go, for we promised to meet Lord Ruskin. If you don't wish to accompany me, I shall take the footman."

Mr. Latham, who'd risen to his feet when the young lady entered, stepped eagerly toward Helen. "I shall gladly offer my escort, Miss Reed."

"And I too," piped Lord Malcolm.

Knowing there was safety in numbers and she couldn't turn her determined cousin from her purpose, Amy rose. "Then Claudius and I shall join you." Perchance she might find a moment alone with Mr. Latham to solicit his help in keeping a watchful eye on her cousin. Maybe even ask his advice on what to do about her suspicions with regard to Sir Hartley. With that in mind, she sent for her coat and bonnet as well as Claudius's leash.

As they awaited the maid in the front hall, Mrs. Reed appeared at the top of the stairs. She hurried down, first greeting the gentlemen, then directing her remarks to the girls. "Helen, pray stay and entertain the gentlemen while I have a word with Amy."

Puzzled what it was all about, the young lady followed Mrs. Reed into the small library which was rarely used except by Amy. "What is the matter, Aunt Vivian?"

"I have come up with another wonderful plan to help dear Helen advance her suit with Lord Ruskin. I intend to arrange a small carriage party to go to Charlcombe. Mrs. Sanford highly recommends seeing the village and the church. We shall invite Lord Ruskin and his cousin to join us." The lady stopped, as if struck by something, and added, "And we must invite your friend Mr. Latham as well."

Amy's heart sank. "Aunt, did you hear nothing I said last night?"

"My dear, I think you have lived too much secluded from Society to understand how these things work. Helen tells me she thinks Sir Hartley is jealous of the earl. That would explain why he is saying terrible things about the man. Besides, I shall accompany you. Nothing can happen while I am present."

"And what of the expense?" Amy crossed her arms, losing patience with her relative who was blind to the earl's faults. "You will have to hire carriages, and provide, at a minimum, a cold collation once everyone returns."

"I have thought of that. Mrs. Sanford has offered me the use of her carriage any time I might have a need. We shall invite Miss Sanford. By including her niece on the outing, no doubt my old friend will be delighted to allow us the use of her conveyance, for the girl is sadly plain and needs every opportunity to go about in company. If we invite your friend Mr. Latham, I feel certain he will provide his coach as well. As to the food, Cook assures me she can provide refreshments that will not shame us."

Amy was nearly at a loss for words at her relative's audacity. She racked her mind what to do, then decided to try another tack. "Aunt, it simply is not done to have a carriage party and expect the guests to provide transportation. It would be a very shabby thing to do."

With an airy wave of her hand, Mrs. Reed dismissed her niece's objections. "Bah, my dear, there is no reason not to accept the kindness of our friends. Dear Mrs. Sanford is well acquainted with our circumstances. Even your friend Mr. Latham has been most forthcoming in offering us every consideration. You know he is quite enamored with our little Helen."

"All the more reason not to take advantage, Aunt. 'Tis too cruel to allow the gentleman to think his suit will prosper when in truth we are taking advantage of his tender feelings."

Mrs. Reed hurried to the desk and began searching for paper on which to write invitations, despite her niece's objections. " 'Tis unfortunate that the gentleman has no title or vast fortune and therefore must be excluded from Helen's candidates, for he is an amiable young man, but, my dear, that is the way of the world. Remember, no one ever died of a broken heart, Amy. Run along with Helen, and I shall attend to the invitations." With that, Vivian Reed sat down at the desk.

Amy knew a sudden urge to shout at her aunt, but all that was likely to accomplish would be to get herself sent away; then who would protect Helen from her own ambition? If she did nothing else this day, Amy decided she must convince Noel Latham that she needed his help desperately. With renewed determination, she went to join the others.

"Well, sir, I can only say that the cat's out of the bag for certain, if you take my meaning." Mr. Henry Baker gazed at Sir Hartley, a defeated expression on his plain face.

The baronet, overwhelmed with frustration, stood at the window of the drawing room staring out at the traffic on Laura Place. He'd been so close to the thief last night, and due to family obligation, he missed his opportunity. He'd actually held the little figurine in his hand and had rushed Miss Addington out of the room so she would ask no questions. "So, I can only assume the news is all over town by now."

"Lord Simmons has been bellowin' about the robbery to all and sundry, sir. We did our best to contain the matter as we did with the other victims, but the baron had other ideas. He's offerin' a reward for the return of the statue or information on the thief."

Hart turned to look at the constable. "What do you think this will do to our quarry? Frighten him out of town?"

"My experience tells me yes." Seeing the disappointment in the baronet's eyes, Baker shrugged. "Still, if he's a brazen one, the culprit might just lie low until all the hue and cry dies down. He'll know everyone will be watchin' for a few days, but after that he can go about his dastardly business. It just depends on how desperate the fellow is for money. I wouldn't give up my vigilance if I was you, sir."

That meant weeks and weeks of more boring parties. Hart sighed at the prospect.

A knock sounded at the door, and Lady Ruskin's butler entered carrying a letter on a salver. "This just arrived for you, sir."

"Thank you, Wilkes." Hart broke the seal, and his face drew into an angry mask as he read Mrs. Reed's invitation.

"Trouble, sir?" The constable peered at the missive, thinking it might have to do with their investigation.

"Something of a personal matter, Mr. Baker. As to our thief, I shall continue to attend as many of the social affairs as possible and be alert to anything unusual. Your men must be on the lookout for the statuette turning up somewhere. Do they have a description of the piece?"

"Better than that, sir. Her Ladyship is something of an artist." The man reached into the pocket of his brown wool coat and withdrew a folded sheet. "Drew us a sketch of the statue which I showed my lads. It's some heathen female fallin' out of her dress. The countess called the piece 'A-fer-dietee Amused.' I call it a waste of good gold."

Hart took the paper and unfolded the drawing. Lady Simmons might consider herself an artist, but he thought she had a highly inflated notion of her skills. It was a rather childish drawing of the statue of Aphrodite he had seen the previous evening. The goddess was seated on a rock, her flowing robes draped so as to expose one breast and a slender shapely leg. He remembered thinking it a lovely piece at the time. "I believe the piece is called 'Aphrodite in a Muse.' May I suggest you have someone with an artistic touch make several copies. Several of your men can show the picture about at the pawn and curiosity shops in the nearby towns, for our thief would be a fool to try to dispose of it here."

The constable agreed, then took his leave promising to inform Sir Hartley if anything new occurred. When the door closed behind Mr. Baker, Hart looked down at the invitation from Mrs. Reed still clutched in his hand. He went to the door and summoned Wilkes.

"Did my cousin receive an invitation exactly like this one?" He held up the blue-edged vellum.

The old retainer gave a nod of his grey head. "He did, sir. Read it, then asked for his hat, coat and walking stick."

Hart suspected his cousin had again gone to meet Miss Reed to accept the invitation personally. Clearly, Miss Addington had not informed her aunt about Silas, or the girl's mother chose to ignore the warning. His first thought was to wash his hands of the whole affair; then he realized that he couldn't. His cousin was young and foolish and might do something now that would taint his reputation for life, not to mention Aunt Roslyn's. Hart knew his own mother would have much to say as well, if she learned he'd stood by and allowed the fool to rush headlong into a scandal.

But what would put a final end to this unsavory business? He'd given up on trying to convince Silas to forgo his plans of seduction. Hart decided he would have at least one more go at convincing Miss Addington that her cousin was in danger and would never be the Countess of Ruskin. With long, determined strides, Sir Hartley left the drawing room and retrieved his hat and coat. He was determined to run the raven-haired beauty to ground and impress upon her the seriousness of the situation.

He stepped out the door as a coach pulled to a stop in front of Ruskin Terrace. The head of his old friend Colonel Maxwell Hensley appeared as he lowered the window, a smile on his rugged, tanned face. The officer looked much the same as Hart remembered him, husky but well built. Sandy brown hair framed a face much weathered from years of soldiering despite his being barely forty. "I see my timing is excellent as usual, Hart. May I offer you transport somewhere?"

"Max, 'tis good to see you. How was your journey to Bath?" The baronet strode forward and shook his friend's extended hand.

"Long and boring, but at least the natives were friendly, unlike my travels in India. Why, I didn't have to fire my pistol once on the trip. And so I am arrived safe but curious. I couldn't resist your intriguing letter. Tell me I'm not too late."

Hart shook his head. "You are in luck. The thief struck again last night, and I'm no closer to finding the villain than when I first arrived. That is merely one of the problems I'm faced with at present."

The colonel opened the carriage door. "Step in and

you can tell me all your troubles while my driver takes us to wherever you wish to go."

Hart gave the coachman directions to the house on Forester Road, then climbed in. He gave his friend not only all the details about the robberies, but his dilemma with regard to his cousin Silas. The colonel asked several questions about the robberies, then seemed to put that subject aside for the moment. He crossed his arms over his broad chest and sat back as his eyes narrowed. "Are *you* smitten with this Miss Reed?"

"When have you ever known me to be bowled over by a mere pretty face?"

"Well, my friend, you *are* growing older." The colonel gave a wicked grin and continued, "No doubt you have begun to think of settling into a comfortable life in your twilight years. Are you certain jealousy isn't the true reason for involving yourself in your cousin's affairs?"

"Dash it, Max, I didn't bring you all the way from Yorkshire to insult me. My twilight years indeed! I'll own that Miss Reed is the most stunning little baggage I've ever encountered. But behind those lovely aqua eyes I've seen little but vanity and a lack of intelligence. Why, if it weren't for Miss Addington, I would be likely to wash my hands of the entire affair, for Miss Reed and her mother seem determined to let my cousin have his way."

"Miss Addington?" Max waggled his bushy brows.

Hart glanced out the window a moment, then back to his friend. "She is Miss Reed's cousin and companion."

Maxwell Hensley stared back at the baronet, a thoughtful expression on his face. "I see." And the colonel thought he did see. Sir Hartley Ross, after all these years, was smitten by a mere companion and he wasn't even aware of the fact. The colonel turned to observe the passing scenery, wondering if he should inform the gentleman of what he suspected, or merely watch the drama play out firsthand. There could be little doubt that the indomitable Lady Ross would be less than thrilled at such a turn of events, if Hart's letters were any indication. He'd written that his mother had thrown nearly every eligible female of the *ton* at his head since he'd inherited from his father.

After giving the matter several moments of thought, the colonel decided that he would hold his tongue—at least until he met this Miss Addington. That decided on, he asked, "Where are we off to this fine morning?"

"I am hoping to have a few words with Miss Addington about this party her aunt is planning. I shall try to find her at home. If not there, I'm certain we shall find the ladies in Sydney Gardens."

"Excellent! I should like nothing more than to view the stunner, Miss Reed." And the lady who'd captured his friend's interest. Max smiled benignly at his friend, who stared at him suspiciously.

Sydney Gardens' beauty drew the residents of Bath each sunny day like a mecca, and this day was no different. Amy and her party had been strolling leisurely about for some thirty minutes before Lord Ruskin appeared. Within moments of his arrival, he'd managed to replace Lord Malcolm as Helen's escort, but to Amy's delight, the younger son of a duke was not so easily intimidated and he stayed tenaciously with the pair.

"I have just come from your home and I gave your mother my assurance that I shall attend her carriage party on Wednesday." The earl smiled seductively at the young lady.

Helen's eyes widened with delight. "We are having a carriage party? How delightful! Did you know that, Amy?"

"Aunt Vivian informed me before we left." She turned to the other gentlemen. "My aunt will have sent your invitations by now as well."

Lord Malcolm cast a soulful look at Helen. "I should be delighted to go, Miss Reed."

Noel agreed to join the party too, but his eyes narrowed as they locked onto the earl. In alt, Helen began to chatter about the proposed trip as she strolled along with her arm firmly entwined with the earl's. The determined Lord Malcolm trotted along beside her. Observing the trio, it was obvious to Amy that the younger son of a duke with little chance at the title was at a decided disadvantage against the suave sophistication of Lord Ruskin.

At last having Mr. Latham alone, Amy allowed her steps to lag, and some distance grew between the couple and the trio. Feeling they had a modicum of privacy, she broached the subject with her friend. "There is something I wanted to speak with you about, sir. It has to do with Helen and Lord Ruskin."

A frown creased the young man's brow, and his gaze riveted on the backs of the group in front of him. "She is only setting herself up for disappointment if she thinks he will offer for her, Miss Addington. Malcolm thinks Ruskin is just amusing himself until he can return to London and the company of his high-flyers."

"I know the earl considers her beneath him in both situation and fortune. Sir Hartley warned me of that recently. But I have the distinct feeling that Ruskin is doing more than merely flirting with Helen."

Latham stopped in his tracks and faced his companion. "What do you mean?"

Amy worried her lip a moment with even white teeth. This was delicate ground. She didn't want her friend to do anything rash such as challenge the earl to a duel. "There was something in the way the baronet warned me that led me to believe that Lord Ruskin might take advantage of her if the opportunity arose."

The stout young man's posture went rigid. "Are you saying he might try to ruin her?"

Seeing his rising indignation, she hurriedly added, "I have no proof, only a feeling. What I would ask of you is to help me keep an eye on her. She harbors the belief that he's falling in love with her, and I wouldn't want her to do anything in the name of love she might regret. She must not be allowed to be alone with him."

Mr. Latham took a deep breath as if to temper his anger. "You may depend on me, my dear Miss Addington."

Overwhelmed to at last have someone to support her, Amy took the gentleman's hand. "Thank you so much. Now that we are conspirators to save my cousin, will you not call me Amy?"

Mr. Latham smiled. "I should like that. I am Noel. Shall we join the others?" He gestured her forward.

As they turned to move toward the trio, Amy spied Sir Hartley and a stranger hurrying toward them. She felt a sudden jump of her heart. Remembering her suspicions about the stolen statue, she became heartsick. Then she reminded herself there was no proof. She had seen him put the little gold statuette back in its proper place with her own eyes and leave the room soon afterward.

"Good morning, Miss Addington, Mr. Latham. Allow me to present my old friend Colonel Maxwell Hensley."

Hart found that he couldn't take his eyes off Miss Addington as the group exchanged pleasantries. Perhaps it was his imagination, but she seemed to be more beautiful every time he saw her. Then he noticed that she seemed to be avoiding his eye. Was it guilt over having allowed her aunt to throw this cursed carriage party?

"Miss Addington, might I have a word alone with you? Will you excuse us, gentlemen?"

The colonel and Mr. Latham moved to follow in the direction of Ruskin, Miss Reed and Lord Malcolm.

"Miss Addington, what can you be thinking to allow your aunt to invite my cousin to this carriage party?"

The young lady's cheeks flamed pink as her warm brown gaze flew to meet his. "Sir, do you forget that I'm a mere companion in my aunt's household? I begged, pleaded and cajoled but to no effect. She is quite determined to bring about a match between the pair and will heed none of my warnings. To her I am an inexperienced young woman without the least notion of such matters."

"Do you think it might help if I spoke to her?"

Amy shook her head. "Helen has convinced her you are jealous of Lord Ruskin."

Hart rolled his eyes and slapped a hand on his thigh in frustration. "I have no interest in that caper-witted chit. Why does everyone seem to think I do?"

Amy couldn't help but smile at his adamance, and a warmth flowed through her at his words. "I didn't say you did, sir. I fear my aunt is a bit blinded by ambition at the moment. She will continue to plan affairs that involve the earl, thinking she is encouraging his suit."

A thoughtful expression settled on the gentleman's face. "Then I think we must make certain that the blinders are removed. Pray tell your aunt that I shall be delighted to come to the carriage party on the morrow."

Amy's brows rose. "What have you in mind, sir?"

He smiled at her with such a roguish grin that her knees grew quite weak. "I don't know, but I feel certain that by tomorrow night, Lord Ruskin's name will be permanently struck from Mrs. Reed's list of suitable candidates for her daughter's hand. Shall we join the others?"

Six

Wednesday dawned sunny and unseasonably mild for a February day as if fate were smiling on Mrs. Reed's plans. The members of the carriage party began to arrive at eleven, and soon the Reeds' small drawing room was filled to overflowing. There were four ladies—Miss Sanford, Helen, Mrs. Reed and Amy—and five gentlemen—Ruskin, Latham, Lord Malcolm, Sir Hartley and Colonel Hensley. The last gentleman had received an invitation upon escorting the ladies home in his carriage from Sydney Gardens two days previously. He'd responded to Mrs. Reed's kindness by offering them the use of his vehicle.

No sooner had the colonel entered the drawing room than he went straight to his hostess and took her hand. "Mrs. Reed, since you have been so kind as to allow me to intrude on your party in this manner, pray let me invite you all to be my guests at the White Knight Inn in Charlcombe. The concierge at my hotel informs me they are famous for their mulled cider and poppyseed cakes."

"Why, Colonel," Mrs. Reed gushed, "we should be delighted to take you up on your offer." She turned to her niece. "Amy, inform Bigelow that we won't be returning here for a light repast after all."

Amy departed to do her aunt's bidding, knowing the

lady was in alt. She'd managed to arrange an entire party without the least expense to herself, but Amy was mortified by all that had occurred. Her aunt simply had no shame when it came to advancing her daughter's chance for making an excellent match.

Returning to the room, Amy noted there was a frosty silence between Sir Hartley and the earl. In fact, they'd moved to opposite sides of the small room. Ruskin stood beside Helen, engaging her in conversation. Observing the pair, Amy could not deny that they made a handsome couple. The earl was devilishly handsome in a grey striped morning coat with a pale yellow waistcoat and grey buckskins, his golden hair neatly framing his face. Helen was glorious in a white lutestring gown with an aqua velvet spencer and matching bonnet.

Amy's gaze veered to Sir Hartley, who stood near the fireplace discussing the points of Mr. Latham's team, yet keeping the earl under a watchful eye. To her, he was remarkably handsome in an elegant brown morning coat over a plain ecru waistcoat with buff buckskins. Then his words from the other day returned, and she was curious if the baronet would make good on his promise to unmask the earl. Yet she couldn't imagine what Sir Hartley would do to change her ambitious aunt's mind, for Amy's efforts had surely failed.

With all the skill of an army sergeant, Mrs. Reed ordered the members of her party to the three carriages she'd borrowed. Her only concern was the placement of Lord Ruskin and Helen together in Mrs. Sanford's carriage; after that, the lady was perfectly content for the others to find their seats wherever they may.

Amy, answering Miss Sanford's questions about Rome, followed her to the colonel's coach, where they were joined by the officer and Sir Hartley. As the baronet sat beside her, he leaned close saying, "I must speak with you in private, Miss Addington."

Her heart raced at the intimacy of the words; then she reminded herself this was in regard to Helen. "I am certain we can find a few moments alone once we arrive in Charlcombe, sir."

The conversation grew general between the four travelers in the coach. Being old friends, the colonel and Sir Hartley told amusing tales about their exploits together. The trip to the church in Charlcombe took nearly an hour, not due to the distance, for one might walk to the village, but due to the traffic in Bath.

Since they traveled in the middle coach, they had to await the arrival of the vehicle that carried Mr. Latham and Lord Malcolm, which appeared to have been delayed. Sir Hartley led Amy behind the colonel's carriage and had a hurried conversation while the others stood admiring the church.

"I have no time to give you the details, but the colonel and I have come up with a plan to show your aunt once and for all that the earl's intentions toward Miss Reed are not honorable. I shall need your help as well as Mr. Latham's. Can you convince him to be party to a bit of subterfuge?"

"I am certain I can, sir." She paused as if she suddenly realized what she'd agreed to and had doubts. "Are you certain no harm will come to anyone?"

He reached out and grasped her gloved hand. "Trust me, Miss Addington. Your cousin might not be well pleased with the revelations of today, but no true harm will occur."

Amy's hand grew warm under the soft pressure of the gentleman's strong grasp as if a reassuring warmth flowed from him to her. "What must we do?"

"I need you to linger at the church longer than Miss Reed prefers. Keep Lord Malcolm, Miss Sanford and Latham with you. I want my cousin to take the young lady back to the White Knight alone."

"Alone?" Amy's eyes widened in alarm, but Hart lifted a finger to her lips to silence her.

"Max and Mrs. Reed will be there, so nothing is likely to happen to Helen in so short a time," he reassured her. "But exactly five minutes after they leave the church, I'll need Mr. Latham to go with me to the inn to take your cousin out for a walk while I have a word with Ruskin. After that, if the plan works, your aunt will know my cousin's true intent."

Amy couldn't imagine what might happen that would change things from how they stood now, but she nodded her head. "I shall do as you ask."

At that moment the last carriage arrived. Amy and Sir Hartley joined the others in front of the church gate. Colonel Hensley stepped close to Mrs. Reed. Taking her hand, he placed it on his arm. "Shall we go make the arrangements for a meal to be served at two while the young people inspect the church?" The widow looked at her daughter standing in conversation with the earl, and doubt seemed to fill her eyes, so the soldier added, "I need a lady's good advice on what one must order for a party this large."

Amy realized at once this was part of the plan. "Pray go, Aunt. I shall look after things here."

"Very well, Colonel." Vivian Reed smiled at the gentleman who was saving her the expense of providing the refreshments.

"If we do not return, meet us at the inn by two." With that, the soldier led Mrs. Reed toward the village. The colonel's voice could be heard echoing back to the group as he informed the lady that he'd once been chased by a tiger in the East Indies, and that didn't scare him half so much as having to order a meal for a large party at an inn.

Miss Sanford, unaware of the unfolding plot, looked at the others and said, "Shall we go see if there is a curate about who can give us a bit of history on the church?"

They filed into the churchyard and stopped several times to discuss interesting headstones that lined the walk to the front door. Some of the markers were so old and weathered that they were illegible.

Helen soon grew impatient. "Can we not go in and see the inside? It is rather ghoulish to be standing over someone's grave discussing how they died."

Lord Ruskin patted the lady's hand that clung to his arm as he gazed raptly down into her beautiful face. "I quite agree. Let us proceed indoors."

While the others moved toward the church, Amy tugged at Noel's arm. "Wait a moment. I must ask a favor of you."

The young man turned, his face a study in discontent at being excluded from Helen's company. "Is there something you need?"

Amy quickly acquainted him with what little she knew of the plan even now unfolding and what Sir Hartley wanted him to do.

Noel was full of questions. "What is he planning? Will Miss Reed be safe? Are you sure you can trust Sir Hartley?"

That last question was the only one Amy felt confident to answer, for while she still hadn't resolved questions about the stolen statue, she believed him to be sincere about helping Helen. "In this matter, yes. He has tried from the beginning to warn me of Lord Ruskin, but I have been unable to make my aunt or cousin listen." She put her hand on her friend's sleeve. "Please do as he asks. I think his plan, whatever it is, will remove the earl from our lives."

Noel's gaze moved to the now empty doorway of the church, the others having disappeared into the depths of the building. A slight smile lit his face for the first time that day. "Very well. I shall do it for Miss Reed's future happiness."

They hurried to join the others. The curate had appeared from the church office and seemed delighted to have visitors in his historic chapel. Learning of their desire for a tour, he quickly began to explain that it dated to Norman times, then told what was known of the early days. Amy scarcely heard a word of the history of the old building. Her thoughts dwelled on how she might keep the others from departing when her cousin was ready to leave. No doubt Lord Malcolm was going to be the difficult one, for he tended to follow Helen about like a loyal pup.

With that in mind, she decided the best thing to do was distract him. She moved to stand beside him and began to flirt rather outrageously with the young man, asking his opinion on every little detail of the building, and agreeing even when she knew him wrong. She clung to his arm in such a manner that even her cousin took note. In normal circumstances, Amy would have blushed to behave so fast, but receiving an approving nod from Sir Hartley made her forget that she felt an utter fool.

Perhaps it had been Helen's rather cavalier treatment of the young lord in the presence of the earl, or perhaps Malcolm was merely flattered by the marked attention, but within half an hour he was wondering why he'd never before truly noticed lovely Miss Addington. He quite liked having a female fawn on him, and with one last glance at Miss Reed's golden beauty, he put the girl from his thoughts in order to concentrate on the exotic raven-haired beauty.

The carriage party had been at the church nearly forty-five minutes when a plump little maid arrived and called the curate away on some domestic matter. The gentleman had no sooner left the building than Helen announced, "I have seen enough. It is quite charming, but I should prefer to go to the inn and rest before we dine."

Amy leapt into action, playing her part. "Perhaps one of the gentleman will escort you there. I am certain that, like me, Miss Sanford and Lord Malcolm would like to look around a bit more and even inspect outside for a while."

Noel glared at Ruskin, then joined the plot against the man headlong. "I shall stay as well, for the curate said that the view from the chapel bell tower is exceptional."

Sir Hartley nodded. "Shall we take a look?" With that, he led Latham to the stairs and the two men disappeared up the spiraling stone steps, not giving Miss Reed a second glance.

For a moment Amy thought that being abandoned by all her admirers might make Helen change her mind as the girl blinked in astonishment at the unaccustomed lack of interest in her wishes. But Lord Ruskin, unaware of the trap, smiled his most charmingly at her. "May I be your lone escort back to the inn? I promise to keep you happily amused until the others tire of cold churches and bucolic views."

Helen beamed radiantly up at him, taking his offered arm. "Nothing would delight me more, my lord." The pair turned and exited the church as Amy bit her lip, hoping that whatever Sir Hartley's plan was, it would work. She struggled to keep her end of the conversation going with Miss Sanford and Lord Malcolm. In exactly five minutes, Noel hurried down the stairs and left the church without a word. Sir Hartley, right behind, paused a moment to give Amy a reassuring nod, then turned and followed young Latham out of the churchyard. She prayed that all would go well and Ruskin would no longer be a part of their lives. Then the disturbing thought flashed in her mind that Sir Hartley would be gone forever as well.

In the middle of the small village of Charlcombe, Maxwell Hensley and Mrs. Reed were inspecting the private parlor of the White Knight Inn. The colonel walked across the room and looked out at the bustling traffic. "This chamber's windows front on the main street. Have you another where there is less noise?"

Mr. Knight's brows rose at the request. The front room was his best, and Quality usually preferred such. "There is a smaller parlor in the rear. But if your party is nine, sir, I feel certain they would be more comfortable in here."

"Let me see the other chamber," Max requested and stepped to the door before turning to Mrs. Reed. "Dear madam, I shall inspect the other room. You stay and rest. I have asked too much of you already."

"You are too generous, Colonel." Mrs. Reed sat down thinking the gentleman all that was proper. It was unfortunate he held no title or vast wealth, besides being far too old for Helen.

The colonel stepped into the smaller chamber at the end of the hall and went to one of the sets of windows, where he opened the latch and looked down. He nearly hummed, the setting was so perfect. "Who does the garden belong to, Knight?"

" 'Tis for the guests staying at the inn, sir. My wife suggested it, and the female guests seem to enjoy the place."

"Excellent, and you have no objection to my guests using it while we are dining here?" Max pulled out his leather pouch and poured a fistful of coins into his palm.

The innkeeper's face split into a grin. "Your guests

may go where they wish, sir. Will there be anything else?" The man licked his lips in anticipation of the day's rewards, his eyes never leaving the colonel's hands as he counted out money.

Since Max didn't know if this was all going to work out as he and Hart had planned, he requested, "Set several rooms aside for the ladies to use, at least for the afternoon." One couldn't drive back to Bath with a hysterical female, and Max didn't know how the Reed ladies would react to having their hopes dashed so horridly.

Once they settled on a price, Max paid the man; then just before he left, he stopped and pointed at the window. "Pray, leave the windows open. This room is a bit smaller and I shouldn't want it to become stuffy."

"Very good, sir." Mr. Knight would have opened every window in the inn for what the gentleman had just paid him.

Colonel Hensley returned to the front parlor and collected Mrs. Reed. Upon exiting into the busy inn yard, he surprised the lady. "I have little interest in churches and graveyards, dear Mrs. Reed. I came for the congenial company and the beautiful ladies. Would you object if we strolled round to the lovely little garden in the rear of the inn that I saw from the parlor window? We can sit in the warm sunshine while I tell you all about my adventures in the Indies."

Mrs. Reed, in excellent humor at her successful party, willingly agreed to the gentleman's suggestion, knowing the others would soon return from the church. She was not a great walker and was quite happy not to have to stroll there and back again. The colonel escorted her down a narrow alley and through a white wooden gate that led into a lovely garden bereft of blooms. The small space held lovely white benches and a small fountain.

Tall yews formed an outer hedge which buffered the noise of the village as well as provided privacy.

The gentleman urged his companion to a bench nearest the building, then suggested that he order some lemonade and biscuits to while away the time until the others arrived. Max hurried back up the alley and told Knight to take refreshments out to Mrs. Reed. But instead of going back to rejoin his companion, he took up a position in the alley to watch the street. At last he caught sight of Miss Reed and Lord Ruskin and ducked behind a post. Max hadn't found life quite so interesting since he was chasing Mughal spies in Calcutta.

After the pair disappeared into the inn, the colonel waited until he saw Hart and Mr. Latham hurrying up the street. He stepped out to meet them. "They arrived a few minutes ago, and Mrs. Reed is in position. It's up to you."

Hart looked to Miss Addington's friend. "Are you ready, Latham?"

The young man nodded, and the two strode into the inn leaving Maxwell Hensley waiting until he was again needed. He just hoped Hart was right and Ruskin would fall into the trap.

In the rear garden, Mrs. Reed thanked the maid who'd brought a tray of refreshments from a rear door, then departed. She wondered what had happened to the colonel, then decided he must have gone to the necessary. As she awaited his return, she leaned her head back against the stone inn, basking in the warm winter sun and the feeling of satisfaction that all was going as it ought. Ruskin had eyes only for her dear Helen and would soon be calling to ask her permission to pay his addresses. She would have to write Mr. Ingram to come and prepare the settlement papers. Helen would become the Countess of Ruskin, and all the snubs and gibes Vivian had received over the years for being plain and having settled for a mere barrister would no longer matter. Her daughter would be the toast of London, giving her entry to the best Society.

The sound of a door closing interrupted the widow's dreams of glory. Then she heard the chatter of two maids bringing something into the room above her. The door banged shut again and the room was quiet. Vivian picked up her lemonade and found it delicious. She hoped everything they'd ordered would be as tasty. That would make her day complete.

Again the echo of a door opening and closing sounded above her. At first the widow thought it was once again the maids. Then she heard the sound of a familiar giggle and her daughter's voice. "My lord, what are you doing?"

"I am going to kiss you, my beautiful dove, before the others come and interrupt us."

Vivian recognized the earl's voice, and her first instinct was to hurry to the room to protect the girl's honor. But she stayed that thought. Why, the man might actually propose to Helen if they were left alone for a few moments. The silence from the room above lengthened, and Vivian began to worry. Then she heard the door open a second time and Helen's gasp.

A man's voice demanded, "Cousin, I would like a moment alone with you. Mr. Latham, would you take Miss Reed out for a bit of fresh air? She appears a bit flushed."

Mrs. Reed could imagine by Sir Hartley's icy tone what he'd witnessed when he'd opened the door. She knew she should go to Helen, but curiosity kept her to her eavesdropping. What would the baronet have to say to the earl about what he'd just witnessed? Would he demand that His Lordship do the honorable thing and become betrothed to Helen?

In the upstairs parlor, Hart couldn't contain his contempt for his cousin, who'd moved to lounge against the fireplace mantel. "You accept an invitation from Mrs. Reed, and then you abuse her hospitality by taking advantage of her daughter. Have you no honor?"

"Spare me your lectures, Hart." Silas yawned, then looked at his nails to see if they were clean. "My position allows me to take what I want." He stared directly at Hart. "And I want Miss Reed to be my mistress. What that scheming mother of hers does is of no concern to me. Perhaps I shall buy the old cat a cottage in the country to keep her happy and out of my hair."

"And you call yourself a gentleman?"

The young man gave a lazy smile and shrugged his shoulders. "Why, I don't call myself anything other than the Earl of Ruskin. That seems sufficient to make up for any deficiencies that one might otherwise find."

Hart, outraged at his cousin's attitude, held his tongue as he walked to the window and looked out. To his dismay, Mrs. Reed was not there. Had she left before Silas had made the telling statement? Would she still not see what was before her eyes?

At the next moment, the door to the parlor flew open. Mrs. Reed entered with her eyes narrowed to outraged slits, her nostrils flared like those of an angry bull about to charge. The lady came to a halt in front of the long table, where her gaze fell on the bottles of wine the maids had only just brought. All she uttered was, "You unspeakable cad. My daughter will never see you again."

With that, she yanked up the bottles one at a time and began to hurl them at Lord Ruskin. Her ire far exceeded her aim, and the earl easily dodged the projectiles. The bottles broke harmlessly on the mantel, the wall, the windowsill and the hearth, but the rich, dark liquid flew everywhere, from the top of the gentleman's crimped blond curls to the tips of his tasseled Hessians. In between, great red blots covered his intricate white cravat, grey wool coat, yellow waist and grey buckskins.

As the gentleman lurched aside to avoid the last flying bottle, his foot slipped on the saturated floor and down he went.

A howl of pain emanated from the earl that sounded like a wounded animal as he landed. Fearing further assault on his person, he cried, "Remove that demented harridan from my sight."

Seeing that all the wine bottles were gone, Mrs. Reed straightened and smoothed the folds of her black gown, then turned to Sir Hartley. "You, sir, had best inform the innkeeper that our meal is canceled and he shall need to have the rubbish swept from the floor." She tossed one sneering glance at the earl. "All the rubbish! I will go gather the others. We are going back to Bath at once. I shall inform Colonel Hensley to remain behind for you and your cousin."

With her head held high, the mere widow of a barrister swept from the room with the air of a queen. Hart leaned back against the windowsill. Crossing his arms over his chest, he smiled at Silas. "Your *position* is a bit precarious at the moment. If you move to the left or the right, I believe you will have a chard of glass embedded in your—"

"Oh, do stubble it and come give me a hand." Silas glared at his cousin.

The baronet looked thoughtfully at the earl, then moved across the room and pulled the man to his feet. As they stood face to face, Hart said, "I hope you have learned a lesson from all this."

The earl gazed down at his ruined clothes. "I bloody well have. It's only champagne for me henceforth. Then if some fishwife decides to hurl it about the room, there won't be any stains."

Hart sighed. Some people were hopeless, it seemed.

* * *

Amy and the others were just exiting the churchyard gate when Vivian Reed, her protesting daughter and Noel Latham marched up to the waiting carriages. Without a whit of explanation, the widow baldly announced, "We are leaving at once. Take your seat in the carriage, Helen, Amy."

Miss Reed turned her tear-stained face to her cousin. "I don't understand. Mama is furious with Lord Ruskin, but I am certain it is merely a mistake."

"Helen!" Mrs. Reed snapped, "We will discuss the matter at home. Pray, forgive the abruptness of our departure, Miss Sanford, but I think that you must accompany us, for your aunt would not be pleased if I left you without a proper chaperon."

Amy asked no questions, only hurried to climb into the carriage, feeling a mixture of elation at Sir Hartley's success and despair that she would be unable to offer him her thanks. Both emotions blended with a great deal of curiosity, but she felt certain that her aunt would tell her what had occurred.

While utterly surprised at the abrupt turn of events, Miss Rebecca Sanford, who possessed little beauty but a great deal of astuteness, allowed Lord Malcolm to escort her to her aunt's carriage, which now held all four women. There could be little doubt that Lord Ruskin had fallen rather abruptly from favor.

Amy lowered the window and begged Noel and Lord Malcolm to call the next day, then sat back. There was a bleakness in her aunt's countenance that filled Amy with guilt, yet she reminded herself that the widow would have suffered far more if Helen had been ruined by the earl. She knew Sir Hartley had done the right thing, but what exactly that was she was curious to know.

The ride home was accomplished in near silence, save the sniffles of Helen. Upon arriving, Mrs. Reed exited, then begged Miss Sanford to convey her thanks to the lady's aunt for the use of the carriage. Without further explanation, the lady mounted the steps and entered the house, calling for the girls to follow. Helen slipped out of the carriage without a word, but Amy lingered to offer her apologies for the strange turn of events.

Rebecca offered Amy her hand, a curious expression on her plain face. "I think you know more about this event than even Mrs. Reed. Is that why you have shown such a devout interest in a rather ordinary village church?"

Amy blushed, and looked down at the cobblestones a moment, then back to the astute young woman. "I do have some hint of what happened, but please don't think badly of me or Sir Hartley. Desperate measures were called for to unmask Lord Ruskin's true nature to my unsuspecting aunt."

"Have no fear, Miss Addington. I have been long enough in Society to know that people are very often not what they seem. I own that I would have experienced some trepidation if the earl had been dangling after a female in my care, such is his reputation. Unfortunately, ambitious mothers too often think their daughters will succeed where others have failed. Whatever happened in Charlcombe I feel certain was for the best."

Amy smiled and squeezed Miss Sanford's hand. "I hope once the dust settles from this uproar that you will come to tea."

"I should be delighted." Rebecca Sanford bade Amy goodbye, then ordered the coachman home.

As she watched the vehicle lumber away, Amy realized that she liked Miss Sanford immensely. The young lady was practical, smart, and her circumstances were little better than Amy's. Clearly, she was a poor relation who lived with her aunt, yet the young lady remained amiable and pleasant. Amy missed the closeness she'd shared with her sister, Adriana, and hoped that she and Rebecca might form a bond, now that her worries about Helen were almost put to rest. However, until her cousin was safely wed, there would be no true peace of mind for Amy.

The thoughts of her cousin suddenly made her realize that Aunt Vivian might have need of her to calm the much distressed beauty. She hurried into the house and straight to the rear drawing room, but she found only her aunt sitting before the fire, looking as if she had weathered a serious illness. Her countenance was drawn into grim lines, giving her angular face an even more gaunt appearance.

Amy went to the lady and took her hand. "Where is Helen?"

Mrs. Reed looked into her niece's eyes, her own filled with pain. "Gone to her room in hysterics, vowing never to come out." The lady gave a shaky sigh; then her gaze moved to the blaze in the fireplace. "He only wanted her for his mistress. He intended to ruin my beautiful Helen."

Kneeling down, Amy patted her aunt's hand. "You now know him for the despicable blackguard he is, and we never need think about him again. Helen is a beautiful young woman, and a true gentleman won't give a fig about her circumstances if he loves her."

"But I thought the earl a true gentleman."

"Aunt, a title is no guarantee that the holder is good or honorable. You must look deeper than mere window dressing if you want Helen to be happy."

Aunt Vivian nodded, then gestured for Amy to come sit beside her. "I think I must warn you that Helen blames you and Sir Hartley for ruining things with Ruskin. She is convinced that I misunderstood what the earl said."

"What exactly happened at the inn?"

Vivian Reed gave a brief explanation of the conversation she'd overheard from the garden between Sir Hartley and the earl. "I fear my outrage was so great that I went up and hurled several bottles of wine at the knave. I didn't land a single one, but at least that man-milliner was a blotched mess by the time I was finished." There was a distinct twinkle of satisfaction in the lady's blue eyes.

"Good for you, Aunt." Amy suddenly wished she'd been there to see Ruskin's defeat.

"No doubt he is more convinced than ever that we are underbred nobodies." The widow sagged deeper into the chair, a defeated expression on her face.

Amy rose and helped her aunt to her feet. "We shan't care a fig what such a dishonorable cad thinks of us. You must go up and rest before you make yourself sick and unable to chaperon Helen."

Aunt Vivian allowed herself to be led to the stairs, but still she had doubts. "But what if he turns the town against us by telling tales, my dear? Helen's chances will be quite ruined."

"Tell tales and let all of Bath know he was humiliated by you? I think not. Likely we won't hear another word from the earl. Besides, remember that my sister is now Lady Borland. I feel certain that Adriana will wish to have Helen come to London with me as soon as she returns from Italy."

The widow brightened. "That is true. She said so in her letter, did she not? But what are we to do in the meantime to convince Helen that her life is not ruined?"

"You leave that to me, Aunt."

Amy got her aunt comfortably settled in her room, then ordered a light meal to be served on a tray. At last she went to her cousin's door and knocked, but the girl ordered her away. She tried the handle but it was locked.

Amy knew that it was going to take time for Helen to accept the loss of the earl as her future husband.

With both her relations in their rooms, Amy went back to the drawing room and settled in front of the fire with Claudius at her feet. She knew that the best way to change Helen's grim mood would be to introduce her to a another titled gentleman, for Amy felt certain the girl's heart had been in no way affected by Lord Ruskin. But where the devil was she going to find a new prospect to dangle in front of her cousin? Perhaps she should go ask Miss Sanford's advice, for she seemed a sensible young woman.

Then one other thought came to her, and she sighed as her hand moved to finger the good luck charm about her neck. She must see Sir Hartley one last time, to thank him for all he'd done that day. Despite the way he made her feel, it seemed that circumstances would keep him from being her heart's desire. Perhaps the charm's luck had run out.

Seven

"Helen has refused to come out of her room for three days straight." Amy watched Mr. Latham beside the fireplace. He'd braced first one foot on the grate, then switched and put the other, trying to dry his Hessians from the drenching they'd taken in the downpour as he'd stepped from his carriage. The weather had been inclement since the day following the excursion to Charlcombe, forcing Amy to postpone her visit with Miss Sanford or to find an opportunity to thank Sir Hartley. "My cousin will only allow our maid, Molly, in and out."

In a voice so low Amy had to strain to hear the words, Noel asked, "Did she truly love the villain so much?"

Amy gave the matter some thought, then said, "My cousin never spoke of love. Only of being a countess. I think it is more the death of her dreams than a broken heart that has laid her so low. She will rally soon."

Noel pondered her opinion as he gazed thoughtfully into the fire; then with a nod of his head he turned to her. "We must do something to lure her out of her isolation and back into Society. No good will come from her sitting there, going over and over her disappointment. A distraction is what we need."

Glad that her friend seemed to be rallying from his

own dark mood, Amy smiled. "I quite agree, but what shall that be? The only invitations we have are to more routs or card parties, and those will hardly entice her to forget her woes after our experiences at Lady Whitford's and Lord Rowland's dull affairs. They were so crowded and boring that we had no one to converse with and didn't make a single new acquaintance."

The young man paced a bit, being careful not to tread on Claudius's tail where the dog lay on the rug at his mistress's feet; then he stopped and shrugged. "I simply don't know Bath well enough to be able to make a suggestion. It's unfortunate that Malcolm is ill today, for he is a veritable talking calendar of events."

Amy was just as pleased that the young man had failed to come. Since the day of the carriage party and her outrageous flirting, Lord Malcolm's attentions had become a bit warm. She'd tried her best to dampen his interest without being cruel the morning after the trip, but he'd taken little note, continuing to send her daily bouquets and lingering at her side when he'd called with Noel.

The butler entered through the open drawing room with the tea tray. He placed it on a table beside Miss Addington. "I sent word by Molly that the gentleman had called, but Miss Helen is still seeing no one, miss."

"Thank you, Bigelow. It is what I expected."

The servant left, and Amy began to pour the tea. Mr. Latham stood watching her and then said, "By the bye, I ran into Colonel Hensley and Sir Hartley exiting a pawn shop in Milsom Street yesterday. They inquired after you ladies and sent their regards. I thought it best to tell them you were all well. Can't think you'd want Ruskin's relative lounging about your drawing room."

Amy's hand had frozen above the lumps of sugar as Noel spoke. "A pawn shop? A place where you sell things for money? Is that not an odd shop for two gentlemen to frequent?"

Noel laughed. "Well, as to that, I think a great many gentlemen have been known to visit those places when quarter day is near and their pockets are to let. I was known to pawn my watch on more than one occasion during my Oxford days when lady luck had forsaken me."

Gathering her wits, she dropped two lumps into his tea and added a bit of milk as she knew he liked it, handing him the cup and saucer without meeting his eyes. "Do you think there might be some stolen items sold in a place like that? I seem to remember my father saying that a great many pilfered things ended up pawned."

"Without a doubt." The young man stirred his tea, then took the seat beside her. "Were you thinking of Lord Simmons's gold statue?"

Amy nodded her head. All her worries about Sir Hartley being a thief had flooded back at the mention of his coming from the pawn shop. It seemed that every time she tried to put the speculations from her mind, some new event rekindled her suspicions.

"A thief would have to be a fool to pawn an article like that in the same town where he stole it. My guess is that statue was taken to Bristol or maybe even as far away as London to be disposed of."

And whatever Sir Hartley was, he certainly wasn't a fool. Still, Amy's conscience bothered her that she'd told no one about seeing the baronet handling the statue at the Simmons's musicale. Taking her courage in hand, and hoping her friend might convince her that her suspicions were foolish, Amy said, "I need your counsel on a sensitive matter."

"You know you may trust me with whatever you wish

to tell me." He reached over to cover her fisted hand with his.

Drawing strength from Noel's gentle clasp, she quickly told him what she'd seen the night of the musicale. "But Sir Hartley put the statue down and walked away as soon as I came into the room. It was still sitting on the table when we left."

A bemused expression came to the young man's face as he pondered her tale. "It might be just a coincidence that he was looking at the exact one that was stolen," Noel said at last, but there was such doubt in his eyes it appeared he didn't believe his own words. "Were you together throughout the remainder of the evening?"

Amy shook her head. "His aunt summoned him, and he took her to her carriage. Then I suppose he went to look for Lord Ruskin. When I saw him last, he was alone." She remembered his reassuring words to her in the drawing room where he'd found her with the earl and Helen. Amy was racked with guilt that she suspected him of the robbery when he'd shown her only kindness.

Noel sat back, a thoughtful expression on his round face. "Well, I suppose we could go to the magistrate with our suspicions."

Amy rose and began to pace. "I could never do that, not after all Sir Hartley did to save Helen from his cousin. I cannot believe that a man with that much integrity would be a thief." A near physical pain gripped her chest at the thought of betraying him. She didn't even want to think about the possibility of taking mere suspicions to a constable.

"Then we shall say nothing to anyone, but I think perhaps we should keep an eye on the gentleman at the next affair." Seeing the look of horror on Amy's face, Noel added, "It's the prudent thing to do, Amy. We would feel like utter fools if it turned out that Ross did take the statue and we'd ignored what we knew. After all, Lord Ruskin has shown us that men are not always what they seem."

Amy slumped down into her chair. She knew her friend was correct, but still the thought of spying on Sir Hartley made her feel uncomfortable.

Noel tapped her arm to draw her attention, she was lost so deeply in her dark thoughts. "Don't look as if you've lost your best friend. We don't know anything for certain. Besides, this is a matter best left to the local constable and his men. No doubt he already has narrowed the possible suspects and an arrest is imminent. We must concentrate on your cousin and her problems. What can we do to entice Miss Reed back into Society?"

At the moment, Amy didn't want to even think about her cousin and her sulks, but that was where her duty lay. "We need someone who can advise us, and who better than the Sanfords? Shall we pay a visit to Queen's Square?"

"An excellent suggestion. If you aren't afraid of a bit of rain, I shall gladly take you there this very day."

Amy hurried upstairs to retrieve her bonnet and cape. She stopped at her cousin's room to try her luck, but from the other side of the wooden door, Helen declined her invitation for an outing. With a sigh, Amy went to see if the Sanfords might have a suggestion.

Amy and Noel were welcomed to the row house in Queen's Square by Miss Sanford and her aunt. Rebecca inquired politely after Helen, and Amy explained about the girl's decline after the events of their carriage party.

"We have something of a dilemma which we hope you ladies might help." Amy looked at Noel, who gave her an encouraging smile to continue. "We think Helen cannot regain her good spirits as long as she is avoiding Society, but Mr. Latham and I don't know Bath well enough to know of some event that would coax her from her room."

Mrs. Sanford, a longtime resident of the city, beamed at the pair. "Why, you have come to the right person. There is little that happens in Bath of which I'm not aware." She grew thoughtful a moment; then a sparkle settled in her eyes. "Mr. Latham, the person you must see is Lady Holmsby, your hostess. The most fashionable event of the Bath Season will be given by her sister, Lady Halifort, in one week. I would guess that an invitation to the marchioness's St. Valentine's Day Ball would entice almost any young lady from her doldrums."

"A ball? Why, that would be perfect." Amy looked hopefully at Noel.

The young man returned the stares of the three women. He didn't have the heart to tell them that his own mother had once aspired to be the marquess's bride and therefore the current lady would have little reason to do him a favor. He played with the spoon on his saucer, wishing the floor would open up and swallow him. If only Malcolm were here—then he remembered that Malcolm was quite a favorite with his aunt. With a relieved smile, he looked up and announced, "It seems Lord Malcolm and I shall be paying a visit to the Marchioness of Halifort, even if I have to prop him up with a Bath chair."

That settled, the conversation became general as the four discussed the dreadful weather and the coming marriage of Princess Charlotte. Amy and Noel politely stayed long enough to finish their tea with the widow and her niece. When Noel dropped Amy at home, he vowed not to return until he had secured an invitation for the ladies on Forester Road. With that pronouncement, he was gone.

Watching his carriage disappear down the rain-soaked

cobblestone street, Amy prayed that he would be successful in his quest for invitations. She was beginning
to worry about Helen. The longer the girl stayed iso-
lated, the more likely she was to convince herself that
she had truly loved Ruskin. Amy felt certain that even
her cousin wouldn't be able to resist the lure of the ball
of the Season. She suddenly wondered if she would
perchance get one last opportunity to see Sir Hartley
there. She truly hoped so.

Hart sat stretched out in front of the fire in Max's
room at the Bath Inn. His mood was as dreary as the
day's weather. The thief was still out there planning his
next robbery, his cousin hadn't spoken to him in three
days, and his aunt was pestering him to know what had
put Silas in such a vile temper. The only bright spot in
Hart's life at the moment was the satisfaction that he'd
finally succeeded in protecting Miss Reed from ruin,
and thereby saving Miss Addington's position as well
as keeping her from the heartache of failing her aunt.

He wondered how the raven-haired companion was
faring. Mr. Latham hadn't been forthcoming about the
ladies when he and Max had met the young man on
Milsom Street. There had to have been some uncomfortable days in the Reed household once Miss Reed
learned about Silas's true plot. She might think her
chances of an advantageous marriage ruined, which Hart
regretted, but it was better that she experience a bit of
disappointment now than to have her whole life ruined.
If only he could see Miss Addington and know all was
well.

"You are rather quiet." Max gazed across the space
between the two leather chairs at his friend.

"Merely doing a bit of woolgathering."

"About a certain young, dark-haired companion?"

The colonel knew he'd guessed right by the angry glare his friend tossed him.

"Miss Addington hardly needs me worrying about her. I have never known a more sensible young lady. She has no doubt been very busy helping her cousin cope with a broken heart these past few days."

Max put his arms up behind his head as he shifted into a lower position. "Do you think Miss Reed has a heart? She appeared all vanity and ambition to me."

Hart's face relaxed into a less grim appearance. "We all have hearts, even my cousin, but I suspect his is rather blacker than most." The baronet had come to realize that his own heart obviously had some dark recesses as well when he remembered the devious way in which he'd manipulated Silas's downfall. But Hart had no regrets. Well, there was one. Miss Addington would no longer be a daily part of his life.

Max chuckled. "Do you think Ruskin has accepted defeat?"

Hart turned the matter over in his mind. He hadn't seen Silas since they'd returned from the White Knight. His cousin had been in a towering rage, breaking a favorite vase and cuffing one of the footmen. The earl hadn't confided to his mother what had put him in such a temper, he'd merely ordered her from the room. Since then, all had been quiet in Laura Place, and that worried Hart. His memories of Silas included one in which the young man had waited a week to take his revenge on a neighborhood boy for having made fun of Silas's seat on a horse at his first hunt. The boy had mysteriously ended up with a broken arm, and Silas's father had been forced to pay a considerable sum to keep the story quiet.

"One can never be certain with Silas. I can only hope that Miss Reed's eyes are finally open, and the ladies won't accept his card or his visits should he be ill-bred enough to call." Clearly, the earl was angry at the turn of events, but might he seek revenge on the ladies? The notion caused Hart to sit straight up, his feet hitting the floor with a thud. He put his empty claret glass on the table. "To be prudent, I think I'll go see if my valet has heard anything belowstairs."

The baronet bade his friend farewell and promised to stop by for him that evening. They were once again to rove through the social events of the evening looking for the thief. It had taken little effort to include the colonel in the invitations, for few hostesses would turn down a marriageable man coming to their party.

On arriving at Laura Place, Hart casually inquired of the butler as to his cousin's whereabouts. He learned that Silas was still in his apartment upstairs. That told Hart little. It could mean that his cousin was up to something, or that he was merely still sulking.

Hart went to his room and summoned his valet. Croft arrived in a trice, and there could be little doubt the aged retainer was full of news as his prim lips quivered with repressed excitement. But the little servant well knew his duty and went about his business without saying a word.

"Well, man, tell me what you learned before you expire from the weight of it."

The valet put the coat he'd selected from the wardrobe on the bed and came to his master. "As you suspected, sir, there's something afoot. His Lordship summoned the head groom to his quarters this morning, then there was a bit of a stir belowstairs when his valet gave orders for all the gentleman's cravats and linens to be laundered at once. Try as I might, I couldn't learn a thing from his man, Waxford, but the upstairs maid thought it might mean His Lordship is to depart."

Silas leaving? Hart suspected they couldn't be that lucky. "Have you any idea where he is going?"

"London, sir. While you were out, I strolled to the stables and chatted up one of the under grooms."

Hart was relieved. Perhaps his cousin had finally accepted defeat. But had he truly given up the notion of having Miss Reed under his protection to retreat to his usual haunts and ladybirds? Very likely, for as lovely as she was, Silas could now have no doubt that her mother would protect her from ruin. "Well, at least he will no longer be a worry to Miss Addington." He wondered if he might go and visit the young lady to tell her the good news.

"Shall I continue to keep watch on the household happenings?" The valet's brows were arched with anticipation at the notion that he could continue to spy on his fellow servants.

Hart's hand stilled as he started to untie his cravat. There was something deceitful about having his man skulk about eavesdropping, but then, his cousin's conduct had been so reprehensible one had to match fire with fire. "If you hear anything untoward, let me know, but don't be plying the servants with questions. I think my cousin has at last come to his senses and knows there are beautiful women tenfold in London."

The older man's face fell as he turned and began to straighten the baronet's personal articles which lay on the dresser.

"You have done an excellent job, Croft."

The valet's face gave no indication he'd heard the compliment, but his chest seemed to swell several inches. "I always do my best, sir." With that, he went back to his normal activities of helping his master prepare for the evening.

Once Croft left, Hart stood in front of the looking glass inspecting his evening clothes. He tugged slightly on his white waistcoat, then buttoned his black superfine

jacket. No dandy, he liked the more sober colors for
evening wear that Brummell had brought into fashion.

Satisfied with his attire, Hart strolled to the fire, kill-
ing time until he needed to go for Max. He fell into a
brown study as he watched the flames. He realized that
with Silas no longer a worry, he would at last be able
to concentrate fully on the task that had brought him
to Bath. He and Max had agreed to attend the Blanken-
brooks' musicale and Lady Chester's rout. Hart hoped
that the thief would once again feel safe, since nearly
a week had passed and the town was no longer buzzing
about the robbery. Instead the gossip centered on Lord
Byron again. News had filled the drawing rooms of
Bath that Annabella, Lady Byron, a new mother, was
demanding a separation from the famous poet scarcely
a year after their marriage.

Hart had it in him to feel sorry for the mismatched
pair and their woes, but at the same time he was glad
something had supplanted the Simmons robbery as the
topic of conversation. Thinking of disparate pairs, he
suddenly wondered if Miss Addington and her cousin
would again join the social activities. He was surprised
at how much he missed seeing those amazing doe-
brown eyes and that lovely smiling mouth.

What could he be thinking? Amy Addington might
have welcomed his help in protecting her cousin, but not
his advances. She would never wish to align herself with
a member of the Earl of Ruskin's family, and he would
do best to remember that the next time they met. He
yanked up his gloves and stalked down the stairs determined to find the Bath thief. Then he could return to his
own estate and put a certain young lady behind him.

Amy had scarcely been home two hours when the
invitations to Lady Halifort's St. Valentine's Day Ball

arrived. She breathed a word of thanks as Bigelow handed her the cream vellum cards. Without delay, she took the invitations and went to her cousin's room. She was determined to gain entry this time.

She knocked, then called, "Helen, I have the most wonderful news."

To her amazement, her cousin called, "Come in, Amy."

She discovered Helen seated at her dressing table. She was fully dressed, and Molly was putting the final touches on the girl's golden curls. As usual, she was stunning. Nothing about her indicated she'd ever been blue-deviled. Her cheeks were rosy and her blue eyes sparkled as she playfully tossed bits of chicken to Sugar who sat on the bed beside her.

"How was your visit with Miss Sanford? She is such a nice young lady, 'tis unfortunate she is so very plain. We must invite her to walk with us in Sydney Gardens once the weather improves." Helen smiled at her cousin before she went back to feeding the pug.

Amy was stunned at the remarkable change. This was not the same girl who'd wept so loudly the day she'd learned of Lord Ruskin's perfidy, then morosely refused nearly anyone entry to her chamber. Puzzled, Amy answered, "That would be very nice. I am certain Rebecca would like that. Are you quite yourself again?"

"One cannot pine over disappointments forever."

Amy was relieved that Helen seemed to at last accept the truth of what her mother had told her. Hopefully, that was the last her cousin would think about Lord Ruskin.

"Molly finally convinced me that I must once again go out and about and enjoy myself." Helen gazed up at the maid with an intense look. "That will be all. You may go about your other business." Then she turned to her cousin as the servant departed. "What is your good news?"

"We have received invitations to Lady Halifort's St. Valentine's Day Ball. Mrs. Sanford tells me it's the event of the Bath Season." Amy held up the invitations.

Helen looked back over her shoulder to the looking glass to adjust a curl. "Then everyone who is anyone in town will be there."

"Very likely. Are you concerned that you might see Lord Ruskin?"

"Not in the least." Helen rose and went to her wardrobe. "Whatever shall I wear? Mother has declared there can be no new gowns this Season."

Relieved that the matter had been so simply accomplished, Amy moved to stand beside her cousin. "This pink gossamer satin. The scalloped rouleau on the hem and the pink rose clusters are lovely. We could put roses and ribbons in your hair as well."

Helen agreed with little fuss, then moved to a chair near the fireplace. " 'Tis so dreadful outside, I am quite content to remain here all day and read a book."

Amy's skin prickled with goose bumps of alarm. That didn't seem like Helen in the least. But as she watched her cousin, she decided that perhaps the girl's disappointment had mellowed her. Amy suggested that her cousin might want to go and visit her mother to lift her spirits, for Aunt Vivian hadn't left her bed since the carriage trip. Amy urged her to try and convince her mother to come to the drawing room for tea. The girl marched off without the least protest, calling for Sugar to accompany her.

Back in her own room to freshen up, Amy ran a comb through her dark curls while thinking about Helen's change of mood. What had made her so agreeable? So docile? She had given her usual sullen reply earlier when she'd been invited to the Sanfords. Yet moments ago she'd seemed nearly her old self when Amy entered the room. More puzzling was her blasé attitude about the St. Valentine's Day Ball and her willingness to wear an old gown with little complaint. Something wasn't right.

Thinking that perhaps someone had paid a call while she'd been out, Amy hurried down and questioned Bigelow, but learned there had been no visitors. Baffled, she ordered tea to be sent to the rear drawing room and went to await Helen and hopefully her aunt, if the girl was able to coax her mother out of the doldrums.

After some twenty minutes, the butler brought the tea tray. He was full of apologies for the delay, explaining that Molly had been away on an errand and had only just returned to help Cook.

"An errand? On such a rainy day?" Amy arched a dark brow doubtfully.

"That was my thoughts exactly, but Cook swears it's nothin' to do with her, and Molly ain't opened her mouth."

Amy suddenly remembered the intense exchange of looks between the maid and her cousin. "I should like to see Molly before you summon my aunt and cousin."

"Very good, miss."

Within minutes, a frowning Bigelow ushered a very bedraggled girl into the parlor, then left. Molly's mob cap lay flat and misshapen on her head. Long wet curls dangled from beneath the wilted ruffle. Her grey wool dress bore two shades, the wet fabric being darker at her shoulders and hem.

"Come near the fire, Molly, before you catch your death of cold."

The servant obeyed without a word. She faced the flames extending her hands to soak up the warmth. A slight shiver racked her body, but she made no complaint, merely waited.

"Molly, where did you go just now?"

The maid half turned, but her gaze remained on the floor. "It were personal, miss."

Amy knew at once the girl was not being truthful by the tell-tale blush on her cheeks. But how best to find out the truth? All servants owned one large fear. "You know my aunt might let you go if she learns you have been taking time away from your duties to meet a young man."

The girl's gaze flew to Amy's face. "There were no young man, miss, only . . . well, I did run an errand for Miss Reed."

"What kind of errand, Molly?"

The maid's hands began to tug nervously at her apron. "Delivered a note to His Lordship's man at the lamppost near the corner."

Amy's heart plummeted. Helen had been in communication with Lord Ruskin. The girl was an utter fool. "Was this the first such note?"

Molly shook her head. "The first one was yesterday. A fellow came to the back door while I was shakin' out the rugs and told me to give a letter to Miss Reed, and no one was to know."

"Did Helen tell you what this missive said?" She knew her cousin would never be able to contain her joy at such an exciting event as a secret note.

The maid nodded her head. "She bragged that Lord Ruskin was beggin' her to believe that her mama had gotten it all wrong. Claims he adored her and hopes she wouldn't be listenin' to the bad things that are bein' said about him. There was a lot of nonsense about her beauty and that was all, but she was pleased as pie. I thought that was the end of it; then the fellow showed up again this afternoon with another message while you was away. This one was full of a lot of rubbishy poetry about her eyes and her hair and how there was no joy in his life as long as she was mad at him. He asked that she send him a letter if she'd forgiven him. I was to take the note to where his man was waitin'."

Seeing the bleakness on Miss Addington's face, the girl added, "I tried to tell her, miss, not to be lettin' him sweet-talk her. Her mama says he's a cad, but she wouldn't listen."

So Helen had forgiven him. That meant that whatever the earl was planning—and one could be certain there had to be something, or why else the secrecy—he could set his plan in motion. "Did the man have a new note for my cousin?"

Molly pulled a rain-spattered missive from her pocket that had Ruskin's seal and handed it to the young lady.

Amy stared at the sealed letter a moment as if it were a viper, then took it. "Molly, don't tell her about this message. Any further missives are to come straight to me. We must do all in our power to protect her from this man. Now go put on some dry clothes and have some tea."

The maid thanked her and curtsied. "You won't be tellin' Mrs. Reed bout me takin' notes to His Lordship's man? I need this position, miss."

Amy smiled to reassure the girl. "I shan't tell, and I'll speak with Bigelow as well."

"Thank you, miss." The girl hurried from the room.

Sitting in front of the drawing room fire, Amy still felt a chill as she stared at the letter. She turned the expensive vellum over and was about to break the seal when she heard Helen and Aunt Vivian coming down the stairs to join her. She hurriedly stuffed the note in her reticule on the table and rose to greet the ladies. Both appeared in better spirits, but there was a paleness in her aunt's complexion that worried her. Whatever was in the note, Amy knew she would deal with it herself. Aunt Vivian would only take to her bed again if she believed that Ruskin was once again a threat to her daughter.

The ladies spent a quiet evening at home. It wasn't until Amy reached the privacy of her room that she at last broke the seal and her worst fears were realized.

My beautiful Helen,
  To know that you have forgiven me has sent my heart soaring. I cannot live another day without you at my side. Come with me to London where I might treat you like the goddess that you are. If you adore me as I you, meet me tomorrow night by the same lamppost, and I shall take you away to fulfill your every wish.

                                                  Ruskin

Amy crumpled the note and tossed it into the fire. Not a word about marriage, but Helen would have failed to take note of such a trifling matter in her delight.

With steely determination, Amy walked to her dresser and pulled open a drawer. She pushed aside the folded clothes and lifted a small pistol. Her father had given each of his children such a weapon while they were still in Italy. The countryside around Rome had been full of *banditti,* and Hugh Addington had thought it a wise precaution to teach his offspring how to defend themselves.

She closed her eyes and wished that her father were here to handle this matter, but he was not, nor was Alexander. She opened her eyes and stared at the well-crafted weapon. She had never particularly liked carrying the pistol, but she had done so to please her father. Now, for the first time, she might have to put it to good use.

Lord Ruskin wanted to pick up a young lady at the lamppost on the corner, and so he would. Only it wouldn't be the one he was expecting. She would convince the cad once and for all that Helen was not his for the taking.

Eight

"Have you taken leave of your senses, Amy?" Noel Latham's voice was an octave higher than normal as he stood in the Reeds' rear parlor the following afternoon, having just been informed of Amy's plan to foil Lord Ruskin's nefarious plot. "You cannot take Helen's place. That libertine is as likely to exact revenge on you for thwarting him as not."

Noel began to pace back and forth, running his hand through his red curls in frustration, mussing the Brutus style he'd so carefully fashioned. He stopped suddenly and put his arms akimbo as he faced Miss Addington. "Why, I should call him out at once. With a bullet in him, he couldn't abduct anyone."

Amy rose and went to him. She'd hesitated to ask for his help, but even she wasn't foolish enough to march off to a meeting in the middle of the night with a scoundrel without informing someone. Ruskin might do just as Noel feared. "Do calm down and listen to me." She led him back to the fire, taking little note as rain pattered at the parlor window. Once her friend was seated, she stood over him, just in case he decided to bolt and do something rash. "You cannot challenge the earl to a duel. That would be almost as damaging to Helen's reputation as her running off with him."

"Well, you've rocks in that lovely head of yours if

you think I'll stand by in the shadows and let you climb into a carriage with that scurrilous dog. You cannot protect yourself any more than—"

Amy held up a hand to silence him. "I won't go without protection. I am not such a fool. I shall take the pistol my father gave me and trained me to use."

His mouth curled into a childish pucker. "I say, it don't seem fair that you can put a hole in him but I'm not allowed. I'd wager I'm the better shot."

"I could hardly miss the man from across the aisle of a carriage, but I am not going to argue with you about who is the better shot—or even shoot the earl, for that matter." She paused a moment, thinking of what might go wrong, then added, "Well, not unless I must. My reason for the weapon was to intimidate him a little. To let him know that unless he leaves Helen alone, I won't hesitate to put a hole in him."

Noel grew silent, evaluating her plan. At last he tilted his head and eyed her thoughtfully. "I suppose there is no way I can convince you not to do this, but to let me or even Sir Hartley handle this matter."

Amy shook her head, her gaze dropping to the floor. "I considered the baronet, but I cannot allow him to further involve himself in our affairs. If things go badly, I wouldn't want him blamed by the rest of his family." She knew that was just an excuse. In truth, she wanted more than anything to turn to Sir Hartley, to rely on his strength and good sense, but she mustn't. He would not be there for her forever. After all, he'd been encouraging her and her cousin to keep away from his family from the very beginning. It was best that she cease turning to him at every opportunity. Noel would be adequate assistance tonight.

Noel rose and took her hands. He gave her a supportive smile when their eyes met. "Then I shall help. But I insist that I be concealed as close to you as possible, and you must promise to call out at once if you have need of me . . . or if you miss the blackguard."

Amy gave an exasperated laugh. "I promise."

"And if things go wrong, then *I* can put a hole in him." There was a determined look in Noel's grey eyes.

Not wanting to give the man *carte blanche* to shoot a peer, Amy asked, "Do you think you could win Helen's heart if you shot the man who holds, if not her heart, the key to all her dreams? She would never forgive you."

Latham, dropping her hands, moved to stand in front of the fire, his back to Amy. "I don't think I shall ever win her heart. She is content enough to be with me until some dashing coxcomb with a title comes along, and then she is off in pursuit of him."

Amy's heart ached for her friend. He'd spoken the truth. Despite all his wonderful qualities, Helen couldn't see past her own ambition and Noel's rather plain appearance and lack of title. "Then why are you helping her?"

He turned and spoke with quiet eloquence. "Because I love her."

Before Amy could say a word, she heard her aunt in the hall inquiring about her whereabouts; then the door opened and Aunt Vivian entered. She greeted their guest warmly, then took her niece to task for having closeted herself alone even with someone they knew and admired like Mr. Latham.

Noel, realizing that Mrs. Reed was unaware of what Amy was about, quickly defended his friend. "I fear, Mrs. Reed, that I am quite the one at fault. I came to ask your niece if there was any chance that Miss Reed might consider my suit."

Vivian Reed's eyes widened. "You wish to ask my daughter to marry you?"

"I do, madam, but Miss Addington has advised me

that the present time is not the best. She thinks your daughter still has not fully recovered from her disappointments of her afternoon at Charlcombe."

The older woman sighed, then sank into a chair near the fire. "That is quite true, sir. She was quite her old self at dinner last evening, but she is strangely in another dark mood this afternoon. I hope this shall pass before the Haliforts' Valentine Ball."

As the trio fell into thoughtful silence, Amy suddenly realized that her cousin was piqued that she hadn't received another missive from the earl. It was for the best that she be on the outs, since Amy would hopefully drive a permanent wedge between them tonight.

Noel made a slight gesture with his head to signal Amy to come outside the parlor with him. "I am certain the ball will lift all your spirits, madam. I have overstayed my welcome, so I shall bid you farewell." He stepped forward and gallantly kissed Mrs. Reed's hand.

"Aunt, I shall escort Mr. Latham out and ask Bigelow to send in tea."

The older woman merely nodded as she sat staring morosely into the fire. Once in the hall, Amy sent the butler off for the tea tray. As he disappeared down the hall, she whispered, "Pray, return tonight at half past ten. We shall find you an excellent place to hide as close to the corner as possible. I shall keep watch, so you won't need to knock at the door and disturb the household."

Noel grasped her hands. "Please be careful. I have a bad feeling about this."

"All will go as planned. Don't worry." She gave a bright smile despite the nervous tingling in her stomach.

The gentleman departed into the stormy afternoon, and Amy returned to the rear parlor. Despite her reassurances to her friend, she was not confident about the outcome that evening. There were myriad things that could go awry, the worst of which was that she might shoot His Lordship, but she wouldn't prematurely worry about what might go wrong, only of accomplishing her goal.

When she settled on the damask sofa across from her aunt, the lady turned an intense gaze on her. "What do you know of Mr. Latham's circumstances, Amy?"

"Very little, Aunt Vivian. I know his father is a diplomat and that Noel traveled much of Europe until Napoleon's rule prohibited that; then he returned to England and school."

"Does he have any prospects, an estate, or even a profession?"

"He has made no mention of any of that. Are you at last thinking him to be a good aspirant for Helen's husband?"

"How can I, dear? I know he would treat her well enough, but good intentions cannot keep bill collectors from the door. I cannot let her throw away her beauty to endure a life of hardship and want."

Amy knew little of her aunt's life with Arthur Reed, but there were very often hints that not only had it not been a love match, but that the lady had been unhappy. It seemed Mrs. Reed had been a far more content widow than wife, at least until the loss of her income.

A part of Amy wanted to argue Noel's merits and the fact that he loved Helen, but at present, her mind was too preoccupied with what was to occur that evening. If all went well, they might finally have seen the last of the Earl of Ruskin. And if her plan failed . . . well, she didn't want to think about such an outcome since she might be facing her own ruin. Fingering the charm necklace, she realized that even the good luck talisman couldn't help her then.

* * *

Silas swung the black tiered cape about his shoulders, then fastened the button as he stood in front of the looking glass admiring the effect. "Has my cousin left for the evening, Waxford?"

The thin valet used a small brush to remove the lint from the dark fabric. "He left with his friend the colonel at eight, my lord."

"Excellent. When he returns, should he inquire, he is to be told I am already abed. Give my mother that note on the dresser in the morning." The earl adjusted the collar of his cape so it arched behind his head, thinking it more dashing that way. His mother was his main worry in this little affair. She had a way of making him feel like a naughty child, and there was little doubt she would be piqued at his sudden departure. His letter pointed out that she had Hart here to act as her escort and he hoped that would be enough. If all went as planned, Silas wouldn't likely see her again before Easter, by which time, hopefully, she would have gotten over her anger at his rather abrupt departure. As to what she might think of his flight with Miss Reed, he felt certain she would care little about the penniless nobody, as she'd called the girl. After all, she had always ignored his amorous dalliances in the past, as any lady of Quality would.

"And if Sir Hartley insists on an audience with you, my lord?" the valet asked as he presented his master with a black beaver hat.

The earl's mouth puckered downward as he angrily snatched the hat from his man. That would be just like his cousin, the damned interfering prig. The man had tried to stick his nose in Silas's affairs since the day he'd stepped foot in Laura Place. Why his mother had found it necessary to invite the man was beyond Silas. Hart had never respected the difference in their stations. It was as if the man thought his superior years outweighed Silas's superior rank. Well, the prosing baronet would find that an earl did as he pleased.

Silas crammed the hat on his head in a fit of temper. "Tell him I am departing for London early and cannot be disturbed. If he wishes to speak with me, inform him to meet me in the breakfast parlor at five on the morrow."

A satisfied smile settled on the earl's face. He actually hoped his cousin did rise at the crack of dawn only to find the parlor empty. That would teach him to interfere in other people's affairs.

The clock on the mantelpiece issued a single chime warning the room's occupants it was half past ten. A frisson of excitement raced through Silas. In scarcely thirty minutes, Helen Reed would be his. A trophy beyond his widest imaginings, so beautiful, so untouched by life. He would take her to London and set her up in the first style of elegance and luxury. Every man in Town would envy him.

"The carriage is waiting, my lord." The valet interrupted his musings.

Silas picked up his York tan gloves, pulling them on as he made to depart. "Make certain to have all my trunks in London by Sunday, Waxford. I shall need my new Weston coats and buckskins. At present I haven't the time to waste on being measured." With that, the young man opened his chamber door. He paused at the threshold and listened. There wasn't a sound echoing in the hall. His mother had gone out with friends earlier, so there should be no one about to see his late night departure.

Still, the earl knew his cousin was not to be trusted. He might return home unexpectedly and ask too many questions. The man was worse than a Bow Street Runner with his prying questions and sanctimonious lectures.

Lord Ruskin hurried down the stairs. The foyer stood empty, so he slipped out the front door. The carriage was waiting, the coachman sat on the box, and a footman held open the door. With a furtive glance about, Silas saw nothing to alarm him on the quiet street. He passed the footman without a word, but paused with one foot on the carriage step, taking enough time to call to the man on the box, "Follow my earlier instructions, John."

A light tug at the front of his hat was the coachman's only acknowledgment before he took the reins in both hands. The footman quickly shut the door and climbed on the perch. Silas was pleased at his men's quiet efficiency on this of all nights.

The carriage began to rumble over the cobblestone streets slowly, then began to pick up speed as they passed through the nearly empty circles and squares of Bath. Silas glanced out the window and noted that at last the rain had ceased. That was good. He didn't need a sodden Miss Reed catching her death of cold. He grinned and propped his feet on the opposite seat. He wished he could see his priggish cousin's face when he learned that, despite his interference, Silas had managed to steal Miss Reed right from under his nose.

Amy drew the hood of the black velvet cloak over her dark curls. She'd had Molly borrow the item from Helen's wardrobe during dinner that evening. She positioned the garment so that her hair and face were shadowed. It would never do for Lord Ruskin to realize too soon that he had the wrong female.

"Oh, Miss Addington, what should I do if you don't come back?" Molly fretted as she tied the sash at Amy's throat.

"I shall safely return, Molly. Mr. Latham will be there

to protect me should anything go wrong." Amy sounded much more confident to her own ears than she felt.

When the servant had finished securing the cloak, Amy picked up her reticule. The small pistol felt heavy in the tatted bag. "Go to bed and try to sleep. Everything will seem better in the morning."

There were shadows of doubt in the young servant's eyes, but she did as she was bade. Once the girl was gone, Amy looked at the clock and took a deep breath before heading to the door. She suddenly realized that Claudius was at her side. She knelt and stroked his head. "You cannot come on this walk." She led the animal back to the fireplace and ordered, "Sit."

Claudius obeyed, but his brown eyes never left her face. The animal seemed to sense her nervousness. She stroked his head again. "Lie down, boy. I'll be back before long."

The dog settled on the rug, but his gaze followed her to the door, and Amy thought she heard a whimper as she slipped down the hall. Downstairs, she went to the front parlor window and stood watch for Noel. The rain had ceased, and intermittent flashes of silver moonlight brightened the night before passing clouds returned the darkness. The cobblestones glistened wetly in the dim light from the nearest oil-lit lamppost. The street was deserted and most of the houses were dark. A chill raced down her spine at the thought of walking about on a lonely street, and she was grateful that Noel would be with her.

After what seemed an eternity, she spotted her young friend's ample figure hurrying down the street. Amy knew there was no turning back now. She slipped out of the drawing room and went to the front door, which she opened stealthily, then stepped into the cold night air, drawing the door closed with a soft click. She shivered as she waited, but she wasn't certain if it was due to the night air or fear of what lay ahead. Within minutes, Noel joined her on the front steps.

"You haven't changed your mind, have you?" Frosted air curled from his mouth as he spoke. The rain had departed but left behind a bone-chilling cold.

"Come, we have no more time to debate the matter. We must find you a good hiding place." Amy slid her hand around his arm, suddenly wishing it were Sir Hartley who was with her in the darkness.

The two made their way up Forester Road. The distances between the lampposts were so great that often the darkness consumed them for brief spells, the flashes of moonlight being too brief to make a difference. At last they arrived at the designated corner, and looked about in the poor illumination of the flickering oil light. There were few places to hide save shadowy doorways. Suddenly the clatter of hooves on cobblestones echoed in the frigid night air, alerting them to the coming carriage.

Noel squeezed Amy's hand. "I shall be right behind you in this arch." Without another word, he stepped into the dark recess of the entryway and disappeared from view. Amy suddenly felt completely alone and vulnerable as she turned to face the approaching carriage.

The dim glow of a lone carriage lantern pierced the darkness. She strained to see the vehicle, but her eyes could detect only the reflection of the lantern in the lacquered surface of the coach. Suddenly the horses loomed out of the darkness, and the vehicle drew to a halt across the street. A footman climbed down and opened the door, lowering the steps. All Amy could see inside were a pair of highly polished Hessians glinting from the streetlight in the black interior.

Her heart pounding, she crossed the street to the waiting coach, reminding herself that Noel was at her back. She climbed the first step and peered into the dark interior, but before she could say a word, strong hands grabbed her waist, pulling her into the vehicle. The door closed behind her. With deft swiftness, she was crushed into the man's arms. Her mouth was ravaged by hot kisses. Her natural instinct should have been to struggle, but to her surprise, the feel of his mouth on hers made her toes want to curl. A strange but pleasant heat seemed to run through her, making her resistance falter.

Amy was brought back to her senses when she felt the man's hand begin to fumble with the laces at the front of her gown. She struggled to pull free, but his left arm tightened about her back as his right hand attempted to explore the soft curve of her breast. Frantic, she drew back her arm and planted a fist in his stomach.

There was a rush of air and a marked grunt as his grip loosened. Amy scrambled to the opposite seat even as she reached into her reticule for the gun. Her palm closed on the wooden grip, her finger found the trigger as her thumb cocked the hammer, and she tried to tug it free of the tatted bag. "Well, my lord, you have mistaken . . ." Unfortunately, the hammer snagged in the fabric at the same time the horses seemed to lurch backwards, throwing Amy hard against the front seat.

"Miss Reed?" a voice clearly not Ruskin's inquired at the exact moment she violently fell to the cushioned seat. To both the occupants' amazement, the discharge of a gun blasted. The explosion of the pistol in the small enclosed area was so loud that Amy's ears rang. The acrid smell of gunpowder filled her nose and closed her throat.

After a second she rasped his name, "Sir Hartley?" A rapidly spreading cold dampness and a radiating pain removed any doubt that the gun had found a target—her leg.

Dazed not only by the shot but by the realization that it was the baronet and not Lord Ruskin in front of her,

Amy tried to stand. "Why are you . . ." A sudden dizziness overtook her and she collapsed to the floor of the carriage.

Hart was horrified as the lady crumpled at his feet. Why was Miss Addington here and not Miss Reed who he'd intended to frighten out of her wits? And where the devil had Amy gotten a weapon? He knelt on one knee, feeling for a pulse, which beat strongly at her neck. A wave of relief washed over him. He'd never meant even Miss Reed to come to harm, and now here he was with her cousin shot on his carriage floor. He lifted her head. "Miss Addington, where are you hit?"

But before the lady could utter a word, the carriage door was wrenched open and Hart looked up into the barrel of a dueling pistol.

"Get away from her, you blackguard." Noel Latham, having lost his hat in his mad dash across the road, stood silhouetted in the lamppost light like an avenging angel, his red curls haloed about his head like hell's fires. He gave a slight gasp as recognition dawned. "By Jove, it's you. You were in it with your cousin all along I should have known that bad blood runs true. You . . . you . . . thief."

Hart's head was reeling. "Thief? Have your wits taken flight completely, Latham? Miss Addington's been shot, and you stand there babbling nonsense. Put that gun down before I take it from you. We must take her home and summon a surgeon at once."

A moan emanated from the carriage floor, and Noel moved back. "Step out of the carriage and move away from her." He didn't lower the pistol, only shifted it aside so Sir Hartley could exit the vehicle.

The baronet stepped to the cobblestone, then turned as if he meant to pull the injured Miss Addington from the carriage floor.

"Take your hands off her, you thieving cad," Latham snarled.

Hart looked back at the seething young man, but there was no hint of compromise in his steely voice. "I can have the coachman knock you senseless and do what I must to help her. Or you can cease your abuse of me until we take Miss Addington home. Once we know she is safe, you may rain your insults on me to your heart's content. But if you call me a thief again, I shall darken your daylights."

Latham looked up to see the crooked grin of the coachman. "The gent's payin' me a king's ransom, so I don't mind levelin' ye to the ground fer the same price."

A soft voice came from inside the carriage. "There is no need . . . for further bloodshed, Noel. Let Sir Hartley help."

"Are you quite all right?" Noel stepped to the doorway.

"No, you silly, I have shot myself. I need a physician."

"But it's all his fault. He's a rogue and"—Noel turned and glared defiantly at Sir Hartley—"as we have suspected, very likely a thief."

Hart was so stunned by the gentleman *and* the young lady believing in the wild notion, he quite forgot his earlier threat to Latham. Instead he directed his remark to Miss Addington. "You think I'm a thief, Miss Addington?"

There was silence in the darkness of the carriage a moment; then Amy's voice could barely be heard. "I saw you with the Aphrodite statue the night of the musicale, sir. Then Noel saw you at the pawn shop on Milsom."

Furious to have her, of all people, suspect him, Hart snapped, "And did you see me pocket the piece?"

Again his question was greeted with a pause before

her reply. "Do you think we could discuss your guilt or innocence at a later time? I don't think my wound is fatal . . . but I am feeling a bit weak and dreadfully cold."

Flooded with guilt, but not willing to let the matter be over, Hart ordered, "Climb in, Latham. We shall use the carriage to take her home. As to your accusations, I have been working for the Home Secretary and the local constable to find the Bath thief. And for your information, there were robberies at Lady Whitford's and Lord Rowland's affairs long before I ever came to town. If you doubt my word, apply to Lord Sidmouth for the truth of what I say."

With that angry rejoinder, he lifted Miss Addington from the carriage floor, so that Latham could do as he was bade.

The lady's arm slid easily round his neck, and she leaned her head against his shoulder. "I was certain it could not be you." With that, she slipped into a faint.

Noel hesitated only a moment before he climbed inside. Hart called the house address to the hired coachman, then with a bit of maneuvering managed to return to his former seat with Miss Addington in his arms. As the coach rolled down the street, silence reigned between the two men.

At last Noel cleared his throat. "I hope you will forgive the accusation about thievery, sir. I can only blame it on extreme discomposure after hearing that shot."

Hart was comforted by the sound of Amy's steady breathing. In truth, he cared little about Latham's mistaken assumption. All his thoughts were on the girl in his arms. "Why in God's name did you allow her to bring a weapon tonight?"

"Allow! Amy Addington is not a simpering little widgeon to be ordered about. She has a mind of her own and a will to match. I did my best, but I couldn't persuade her to let me handle matters. But what the devil were you doing here instead of the earl?"

"Trying to frighten some sense into Miss Reed." Knowing what an innocent Miss Reed truly was, he'd thought showing the girl what a man of passion expected might waken her to the dangers of her situation. But it had been Miss Addington he'd kissed. Then he remembered the taste of her warm mouth on his, as well as the soft feel of her feminine body, and he felt an utter beast. He hoped that she would understand and not take offense. If only she would be all right, he would beg her pardon.

Noel interrupted the man's musings. "I don't understand. Where is Lord Ruskin?"

"I believe Colonel Hensley should have driven him halfway to Marlborough if he hasn't overturned the man's coach in a ditch. Max never could drive a coach and four very well, but he insisted he must play John Coachman in this little farce." Feeling a shiver rack her, Hart pulled Amy's cloak tighter around her as the coach drew to a halt. "Everything would have gone off without a hitch if you and Miss Addington hadn't turned the tables."

The footman opened the door, and Noel jumped out and began hammering on the knocker. Hart handed the unconscious woman to the footman, then, once out of the coach, took her back.

There was a long interval before Bigelow, in nightcap and an elegant blue banyon that must have belonged to his late master, opened the front door to see two familiar gentlemen standing on the stoop. Befuddled with sleep, the old man was puzzled until he lifted his light to see Miss Amy in Sir Hartley's arms.

Hart, hoping to awaken the old man from his sleepy lethargy, barked, "We need a surgeon at once. Miss Addington has been shot."

Before the servant could utter a word, a loud shriek rang out in the foyer. Bigelow stepped aside, and all could see Mrs. Reed, who unbeknownst to anyone had slipped downstairs to see who had paid a late night call, and now lay sprawled in a swoon on the foyer rug. But the old man knew where his duty lay first. Ignoring the supine Mrs. Reed, he said, "Put Miss Addington in the last bedchamber at the rear of the hall. I shall send Peter for the physician at once."

After closing the front door, Bigelow tossed one worried look at his mistress, then went to the servants' quarters to waken the footman. Hart stepped over the supine lady and carried Amy upstairs, with Noel following behind. The younger man dashed down the passageway to open the door to the designated room, then hurried in and drew back the covers.

Hart gently laid the injured lady on the bed. In the dim light of the candles beside the bed, she looked so small and vulnerable that he wanted to take her in his arms once again and will the liveliness back into her lovely face. Wishing a few minutes alone with Miss Addington, he looked up at a very concerned Noel. "Perhaps you should go to Mrs. Reed. There is nothing we can do here until the surgeon comes." With a last look at Amy, the young man reluctantly agreed and exited the room.

Claudius rose from the fireplace rug and padded to Sir Hartley's side, jumping up with his front paws to sniff at his mistress. The animal uttered a low whine.

Stroking the dog's head, Hart said, "She'll be fine, boy. Go back and lie down."

But Claudius wasn't leaving Amy's side. He settled on the rug beside the bed.

Hart took Amy's hand and was reassured when her fingers curled around his. "Amy, can you hear me?"

"I-I'm so c-cold." Her voice was weak as her eyes fluttered open.

He tugged the covers back over her, heedless of her boots and blood-stained gown. "There, that should help."

"Am I going to . . . die?" A hint of fear tinged her voice.

"Of course not." Hart knew in that moment that he couldn't bear it if this lovely creature perished. Without giving the matter a moment's thought, he sat on the bed and took her in his arms, blankets and all. "It's only the cold making you feel so weak. 'Tis less of a wound than many soldiers received at Waterloo, and they are alive and well." In his own mind, he told himself he wouldn't let her die.

She sighed and nestled into his hold. Suddenly her eyes flashed open and she drew back as her awareness returned. "What were you doing in Lord Ruskin's coach?"

"Don't worry about that for the present. I'll tell you everything once the doctor has seen to your wound."

"I want to know at once. If you hadn't mauled me so abominably in the coach, I wouldn't have tried to pull my gun." Temper brought color to her too pale cheeks.

Hart realized that Mr. Latham was right. This young lady had a mind of her own. On impulse, he tilted up her chin and kissed her willing mouth. The moment seemed to go on forever, but when it was ended it seemed far too short. Amy sighed and melted into his arms.

"Was that so abominable, my dear?"

She shyly gazed into his eyes. "Of course not, but—"

Hart put his fingers across her lips. "Suffice it to say, we were both trying to protect your cousin. You by taking her place, me by frightening some sense into her."

The door opened and a portly grey-haired gentleman, with waistcoat unbuttoned and cravat hastily tied in a crooked knot, was ushered in by Bigelow. Molly trailed behind, sniffling. "This is Dr. James, Sir Hartley."

Without a word to the others, the physician went to the bed. "Bigelow, take some hartshorn and water to your mistress. Hers is just a swoon."

"Very good, sir." The butler disappeared out the door.

"Girl," Dr. James called the maid, "bring me a branch of candles. I must be able to see to work."

Molly went into the hall and soon returned with a small pewter candelabra, and set about lighting the unlit tapers.

While he awaited better lighting, the doctor tossed back the covers, then paused, glaring at Sir Hartley. "Unless you are this female's husband, I suggest you leave. I shall come and inform the family how the patient is doing once I have taken care of her." Then as an afterthought the physician pointed to the rug. "And take that dog with you. He's in the way."

Hart wished Amy were his wife at that moment so he wouldn't be forced out. But he couldn't claim that right, so he picked up Claudius and carried the dog into the hall.

"Close the door, sir." the doctor barked.

Reluctantly the baronet closed the portal, then sat Claudius in front of the door. The animal sat down and, like Hart, stood staring at the white wood.

The only thought ringing in Hart's brain was that Amy must return to good health.

Hysterical shrieking filled the hallway. Hart froze, then realized the source of the sound to be the front hall. The babble of words held no meaning, but it was Helen Reed yelling. Hart knew a sudden urge to throttle

Lynn Collum

the girl, for without her silly ambition, none of this would have occurred. He strode down the hall, leaving Claudius to stand vigil. The baronet intended to give Miss Helen Reed a piece of his mind and finally set her straight on the matter of the Earl of Ruskin.

Nine

Sir Hartley halted at the top of the stairs and surveyed the scene below. He was too tired and too worried about Miss Addington to involve himself in the contretemps going on in the Reeds' small foyer. Mr. Latham could handle the volatile miss, since that was what he seemed to desire.

Below, Noel held his arms crossed in front of his face as the hysterical Miss Reed pummeled him and shrieked a lot of nonsense. In truth, one could make no sense of her babble of words, but her actions were clear.

"Do calm down, Helen, and listen," Noel managed to utter when the distraught girl paused to take a breath.

But Miss Reed's nerves had been pushed beyond the breaking point. Every wrong, every hurt and every disappointment of the last month appeared to have come to the surface upon seeing her mother lying on the rug. Without the least remorse, she was taking out her frustration on Mr. Latham. At her feet the small pug joined in the assault, nipping and barking at the man his mistress had chosen to savage.

"I won't listen, you beast!" Helen ranted, pummeling the young man.

"Do you not wish to know the truth?" Noel asked in frustration.

Bigelow returned to the hall at that moment with the

items the doctor had ordered. At a loss about what to do in the face of Miss Reed's discomposure, he merely stated to the room at large in a voice loud enough to overcome Helen's tirade, "The hartshorn and water Dr. James ordered for Mrs. Reed."

Noel eyed the old man as if he'd taken leave of his senses. The abused young man's gaze fell on the bottled ammonia and glass of water as Helen's fists continued to pummel him. Without a thought but to bring the young lady to her senses, he snatched the glass and dashed the water in Miss Reed's face. Stunned silence reigned in the foyer.

Helen stood ramrod stiff with droplets of water running down her horrified face, her arms in the air like a bird frozen in flight. The golden curls peeking from her nightcap were pasted to her face as water dripped from her chin onto her wrapper. Noel knew he must act quickly. He grabbed her arms, pinning them to her sides as he gave her a gentle shake. "You shall listen to me. Your mother has merely fainted. She is not ill or in any way harmed."

"You threw water in my face." Outrage narrowed Helen's eyes as she glared at Mr. Latham.

"I did, to force you listen. Mrs. Reed will be fine. 'Tis your cousin—"

"How dare you throw water in my face?" Helen couldn't seem to get past that single fact. Her countenance grew pink with anger.

Noel shook her a second time. "And I shall do so again unless you pay heed to me. Your cousin has been *shot.*"

Helen's eyes widened. "Shot?" As his words finally penetrated the young lady's self-absorbed anger, her lips began to tremble. "But how? Is she dead?" There was genuine fear for Amy in the young lady's aqua blue eyes.

Descending the staircase, Sir Hartley answered the question. "The doctor is with her now, but it doesn't appear to be a fatal wound."

Noel looked up, relief washing over his face to hear the baronet saying such things. It allayed much of his guilt. He'd failed Amy tonight and would never have been able to cope with that failure had she expired.

Helen's trembling hand rose to push back her wet curls. "How did this happen? She retired to bed the same time as Mama and me."

Realizing that they'd finally gotten through to her, Noel released her arms and pulled a handkerchief from his pocket and began to gently dry her face. "It is a very long story, but I think we must see to Mrs. Reed first."

Helen's gaze dropped to her mother, who lay at their feet. "You are quite right."

She took the bottle of hartshorn from the tray and pulled the stopper from the top. Kneeling, she waved the pungent liquid under the lady's nose. Mrs. Reed's eyes fluttered open and she peered at the four people standing over her. Dazed at first, she sat up, looking about her as she straightened her cap and tugged at her pink wrapper. Seeing that she was in the foyer, she frowned, but soon her eyes widened in horror as her memory returned. The lady burst into tears. "W-where is my dear niece? D-do tell me how badly she is shot."

The baronet quickly informed the widow her young niece was in the capable hands of the local physician. Sir Hartley and Mr. Latham then helped the lady to her feet and ushered her to the rear parlor. A subdued Helen, having scooped Sugar into her arms, sent Bigelow for tea while they waited to hear Dr. James's verdict on Miss Addington's condition.

After a sustaining sip of the warming amber liquid, Mrs. Reed glared at the two young gentlemen. "Tell me how this dreadful thing happened. Why was my niece out at this hour, and how was she shot?"

The men exchanged guilty glances, but Sir Hartley made the explanation. His eyes narrowed as his gaze settled on the young lady still clutching her dog. "It seems that my cousin has been carrying on a secret communication with your daughter."

The widow turned to look at Helen with horror. "How could you do anything so foolish when you know what the man intends?"

Helen's chin rose indignantly. "He loves me and wants to take care of me. To him I am the most beautiful creature he's ever seen."

"And clearly quite the most addlebrained." Noel's ire boiled over. "Did you think we were all merely trying to ruin your chances when we told you his intentions weren't honorable?"

Tears filled Helen's eyes as she glanced at each angry face that glared back at her until she finally came back to Mr. Latham's ruddy countenance. "I-I thought . . . oh, I don't have to explain anything to you." She turned her back on the young man and stared into the fire, sniffling.

Hart put a hand on Noel's arm as the young man's own anger choked him. The baronet was determined to drive home the point that so far had escaped the silly chit. "Lord Ruskin very likely does love you, Miss Reed, just like all his other mistresses. They all live in the first style of elegance . . . until he tires of them and passes them onto one of his friends."

Helen gasped and put the pug aside, rose to face the lot of them. "Mistress! You are *all* wrong. He wants me to be his wife."

Hart moved to stand in front of the misguided girl. His irritation fled in the face of her naive tears, and he felt only pity for her. "Silas told me the first day of his meeting with you at Sydney Gardens that you were to be his next mistress. He collects beautiful women just like some men collect books or art. Your circumstances led him to believe you would be willing to accept his offer. I fear my cousin is an unmitigated cad, my dear."

Tears spilled freely down Helen's pale cheeks, and she looked from one gentleman's face to the other. There could be no doubt that at last she had accepted the truth. She collapsed into the chair, dropping her head and weeping in earnest. Noel's face softened, and he moved to sit beside her, taking her in his arms.

Mrs. Reed eyed the pair with doubt as her daughter nestled into the young man's willing arms, but did nothing to interfere in Mr. Latham's comforting. Instead she turned to Sir Hartley. "I still don't understand how Amy came to be wandering about at this time of night and shot."

Sir Hartley quickly explained about discovering his cousin's plot to take Helen to Town at the last minute. With Colonel Hensley's help, they'd waylaid Ruskin's servants, and Max had taken the earl east instead of bringing him to Forester Road. Hart had hired a carriage and made the rendevous. "Unfortunately, Miss Addington had discovered the secret correspondence and took Helen's place to let Lord Ruskin know that his plot was foiled. For any further details about her involvement, you will have to question Mr. Latham. I believe he was her confidant in the matter."

Hart experienced a momentary twinge of jealousy. Why had Miss Addington not turned to him? It would have saved them all a great deal of pain and worry. He eyed the young man who sat beside Miss Reed. Latham spent a great deal of time here with the ladies. Had Amy developed a tendre for a young man foolish enough to fall in love with her hen-witted cousin? A coldness ran through Hart's veins. Had he waited too long, been too concerned with protecting Miss Reed, so that Amy's affections were engaged elsewhere? Then he remembered the warm response to the kiss they'd just shared. She must feel some affection for him. He held on to that hope.

Realizing that Mrs. Reed sat staring at him, awaiting a full explanation, he added, "As to the injury, your niece tried to remove a pistol from her reticule. It discharged in the carriage and wounded her."

Vivian Reed turned her glare on Mr. Latham. "What can you have been thinking to give my dear niece a weapon?"

"I gave her nothing but good advice, ma'am."

Helen drew back from him, managing to get her emotions under control. "You tried to help me?"

His voice softened as he gazed into the young lady's glistening eyes. "I tried to tell her to let me or Sir Hartley manage this affair, but she would have none of it. She wanted to save you." Then as an afterthought, he looked at the widow. "The pistol was hers, madam, a gift from her father."

The sound of footsteps on the stairs caused all the people in the room to turn toward the door. Bigelow ushered the doctor into the parlor.

"Miss Addington shall be fine. It was only a minor flesh wound that is rather long, running the length of her lower limb, but not deep. After a few days' rest she can once again come downstairs, but she must limit her activities. I have given her something to help her sleep."

A murmur of relief went round the room. Mrs. Reed graciously offered the physician some refreshment, then plied him with questions about the care of her niece. Even Helen asked what she could do to help.

Hart only half listened as the talk turned to the patient's diet. He wanted to go to Miss Addington, see for himself that she was well, but he knew that Mrs. Reed would deny him access tonight. At least he had the peace of mind of knowing she was safe. Then he suddenly realized that his work was not done. He needed to go to Max's inn and make certain the colonel had managed to survive Silas's anger once he learned he'd been duped. A smile tipped his mouth at such a notion. More likely, Silas was the one who'd been in danger if he'd dared to challenge a hardened campaigner like Hensley.

"Sir Hartley," Mrs. Reed snapped, "I cannot think what there is to be amused about in this horrid affair."

"Why, madam, have you given Lord Ruskin a single thought? I should have liked to have been there when he discovered that instead of a lady's soft kiss to awaken him, there was the colonel's hard fist."

A look of satisfaction settled on the widow's angular features. "Quite so."

Realizing the lateness of the hour, Hart said, "Doctor, Mr. Latham, perhaps we should leave the ladies to retire."

The gentlemen departed, but not before Sir Hartley and Noel begged permission to visit the following afternoon and the doctor promised to come and see how the patient was doing. Mrs. Reed agreed, thanking the men for their help.

Hart offered both gentlemen a ride in his hired carriage. Once the doctor had been delivered to his residence and the two men were alone in the carriage, Noel asked, "Do you think your cousin will have finally put Helen from his mind?"

"I think that, more importantly, the young lady has put Silas from hers. She is no longer vulnerable to his charms." He heard Noel give a satisfied sigh, but Hart didn't know if that meant the young man's chances were any better than they had been a week ago. Miss Helen

Reed had given up on the Earl of Ruskin, but had she given up on snagging a title and fortune? Hart doubted she had. There was a great deal of truth to the adage that a leopard didn't change its spots.

Noel interrupted his thoughts. "Where do you plan to stay? I cannot think Lord Ruskin will welcome you home after this night's work."

Hart arched one brow. In the mad rush to foil Silas, he hadn't given a thought to the matter. His cousin would be furious if he did return to Bath. "I suppose I shall move into the inn where Max is staying."

The young man fidgeted a bit in the dark carriage, then asked, "If you have no objections, I should like to help you with your task of finding this thief. I think it's the least I can do after so rudely accusing you of the crime and without the least proof."

Hart laughed. "I should welcome any help you might offer." They fell to discussing a plan of action. At last the carriage arrived at the Duke of Holmsby's house in the Royal Crescent and the two men said their farewells.

As the carriage passed once more through Bath, Hart realized that more than one good thing had come from this night's work. Not only was Silas no longer a threat to Miss Reed, but Hart had enlisted another pair of eyes to help him watch for the Bath thief. He'd also come to realize his deep feelings for Miss Addington. Now all he had to do was hope the young lady held the same emotions for him.

A slow, warm feeling of drowsiness crept over Amy as she lay in her bed. Her leg hurt, but she didn't want to surrender to the effects of the laudanum. She wanted to savor the kiss she'd shared with Sir Hartley. Not the hot, punishing kisses in the carriage, but the sweet, tender one here in her room.

"Miss Addington, is there anything you wish afore I bid you good night?"

Amy's eyes fluttered open, and she saw Molly at the door, clutching the blood-soaked gown, stockings and towels used to clean and bind her wound. "That will be all tonight."

"Do you want I should stay with you, miss? I don't mind sitting in that chair all night."

Amy was touched by the maid's kind offer. "That won't be necessary, Molly. You heard the doctor. I shall be up and around in a few days. For now I only need sleep, as do you. I've kept you up late enough for one evening. Just put those clothes in cold water to soak and retire to your bed."

The maid curtsied and left.

Amy settled back once again to ponder the significance of Sir Hartley's kiss, but a knock at the door halted that pleasure. Without waiting for a summons, the door opened and Helen stuck her head in. "Molly said you were still awake. Do you mind if I come in for a few minutes?"

There was something so chastened in her cousin's tone, Amy didn't have the heart to send her away. "Do come in."

Helen entered and came to stand beside the bed. Her reddened eyes seemed to gaze everywhere but at her cousin as her teeth nipped at her lower lip. At last she stuttered out, "C-can you ever forgive me for being the ninny I so vehemently denied I was?"

With a soft laugh, Amy realized that for the first time she might be seeing the real Helen, not the one her mother had created with plots and plans. There was something so human about her at this moment that Amy knew she truly liked her cousin even with all her faults. "Not a ninny, dear Helen; just blinded by ambition."

"I have been so horridly vain and selfish. I behaved

as if my beauty would open any door, quite forgetting that birth and fortune count for more in Society." The girl sighed, and a single tear rolled down her face.

Convinced that Aunt Vivian was much to blame for Helen's conduct, Amy had no trouble forgiving her. She took the girl's hand. "Don't let Lord Ruskin's despicable conduct turn you against all Society. While we lack fortune, there can be little doubt that Addington blood is quite as blue as that of any aristocratic member of the *ton*. No true gentleman would be ashamed to introduce you to his family. True love can open many a door."

Helen brushed away the tear and gave a half smile, then leaned over to kiss her cousin's cheek. "I won't keep you up all night chattering about what a fool I have been. You need your rest. I shall leave your door open and mine as well. Simply call if you have need of something."

Amy bade her cousin good night. As Helen left the door open, the sound of paws pattered on the floor; then Claudius's head appeared at the side of the bed. Amy reached out and stroked him.

Helen stopped, looking back. "Do you want me to take him to the kitchen? He is likely to disturb your rest tonight."

"That won't be necessary. He's always quiet."

After her cousin went into her own room, Amy patted the side of the bed and the hound sprang up and nestled next to his mistress. "Good boy."

Amazed at the change in Helen, Amy decided that all tonight's worry and pain had been worth the trouble. Hopefully, the girl would at last look for love and not worry about social standing and great wealth. As she went over their conversation in her mind, she suddenly wondered how much truth there was in her statement. Would a gentleman disregard their straitened circumstances to offer marriage? More specifically, did Sir

Hartley's feeling go deep enough to consider marriage to a girl without a dowry? Or had that kiss been one of guilt after her accidental shooting?

The question was not to be resolved in her mind that night as the sleeping potion finally took hold. Her last thought was to wonder if the baronet would pay her a visit on the morrow.

Amy didn't see Sir Hartley for the next two days. While the gentleman and his friend the colonel called each morning, Mrs. Reed adamantly denied them access to her niece's room, saying it wasn't proper. Amy's days, however, were not without reward. Helen spent a great deal of time in company with her cousin, and the young ladies finally got to know one another as family should. They read to each other, talked about the hardships of their childhoods and confided their dreams. To Amy's surprise, Helen truly desired a house in the country with a gentleman who loved her, having spent her life in London with a distant father.

"Then why have you been so adamant about marrying a titled, wealthy gentleman?" Amy's brow's drew together in puzzlement.

Helen propped her chin up on her hand and gazed out at the grey day. "Because it has been Mama's wish as long as I can remember. You cannot imagine the sacrifices she has made for me. Every cent she could find she put into dancing instructors, pianoforte lessons and the finest gowns. She said I had a duty not to squander my beauty."

"But is not happiness important as well?"

Looking at Amy, Helen shrugged her delicate shoulders. "For her, those things must represent happiness." Then she looked down at her hands. "There was a young man once, a clerk in my father's office who I liked. Mama grew so agitated because I had encouraged him that I thought she would do herself an injury. I don't want to ever see such a look on her face again."

Amy leaned forward, taking her cousin's hand. "Don't let Aunt Vivian's dreams become yours. I am here to help her accept your choice, whatever that may be. My parents had little money but a great deal of love and happiness despite all our hardships in Rome."

Helen shook her head doubtfully, but Amy cut her off before she could speak. "At least, promise me you won't rush into anything with another titled gentleman."

"I promise I shall take my time with the next gentleman I meet."

Not wanting to push the point, Amy changed the subject. She questioned her cousin about Lord Borland, Adriana's husband, but Helen knew little of the man other than that he was a noted book collector. That made Amy's eyes widen; then she laughed heartily, for she knew Adriana was not bookish in the least. It seemed that opposites did attract.

Opposites. That would certainly describe her and Sir Hartley. He was one of Society's elite, a Corinthian, and she was a penniless companion. Was that something love could overcome?

Amy blinked twice. Why, she did love Sir Hartley! The realization made her feel warm inside. It was also a secret she had no intention of sharing with her cousin. Caught up in the heady emotion, she begged fatigue, and Helen left. Alone, Amy suddenly realized that while she was certain of her feeling, she had no idea of Sir Hartley's. Did the gentleman hold some tender emotions for her? If so, would they be enough to allow him to defy his own family and marry for love? As she nestled into her covers, she knew that only time would tell.

On the third day of Amy's convalescence, Dr. James pronounced the young lady well enough to be up and about. After a light luncheon in her room, she made her way to the rear parlor. Aunt Vivian had a sofa moved near the fire and insisted that her niece recline there covered with a light blanket, despite the young lady's protest that it wasn't necessary.

To Amy's surprise, a steady stream of visitors began to call. It appeared that her aunt had sent their regrets to several of the parties they were to attend over the past several days, saying that her niece had been felled with a case of ague. Mrs. Sanford and her niece arrived first to visit the recuperating patient.

"Why, my dear Miss Addington, you are still looking quite pale." The lady then turned to Mrs. Reed. "Tell me, does this mean that you shan't attend Lady Halifort's St. Valentine's Day Ball?"

"Well, I had not thought so far in advance, what with everything that has happened."

Mrs. Sanford's eyes lit, ever ready for any tidbit of gossip. "What, did something unusual occur?"

Both the Reed ladies sat speechless, but Amy calmly replied, "Aunt merely means my sudden illness, ma'am." Knowing how important it was to Aunt Vivian to have Helen moving in Society again, Amy added, "As to the ball, I feel certain I shall be quite well enough to go."

Aunt Vivian, gathering her wits, nodded. "If you think you can, my dear. But I must insist, no dancing for you." The widow's gaze dropped to Amy's wounded leg.

Rebecca Sanford smiled and patted Amy's hand. "I rarely dance, so I shall gladly sit with you."

Amy was about to protest the prohibition on dancing when the door knocker sounded. After all, it was her first ball; then she realized that perhaps her aunt was right. But to sit against the wall with all the dowagers and spinster held little allure.

Minutes later, Bigelow ushered Sir Hartley and Mr. Latham into the small rear parlor. When Amy's gaze met the baronet's, she suddenly felt shy, but the answering twinkle in the gentleman's eyes reassured her. Suddenly she had an idea. She knew what she could do at the ball, but she would have to ask Sir Hartley's permission to join in his hunt for the thief.

That proved impossible as long as Mrs. Sanford and her niece were present. The elder lady plied the gentlemen with questions. First she queried Mr. Latham about Lord Malcolm's continued ill health and was assured that he, too, was well on the mend. Then she turned her curiosity on the baronet. "I understand Ruskin has departed rather abruptly. That is most unusual, for generally he stays with his mama until Parliament opens."

Sir Hartley arched one brown brow and rather frostily replied, "I believe business called him to London, ma'am. I fear ladies forget that we gentleman have estates to run."

There could be little doubt the gentleman's tone would allow no further discussion on the topic of his cousin. A speculative look settled in Mrs. Sanford's eyes. The lady was well aware of Mrs. Reed's hopes in regard to a match between Ruskin and Helen, but she said no more on the subject.

Mrs. Reed, nerves on edge that the scandal of Amy's escapade would become known, rose suddenly and announced, "Come, Helen, let us open the doors between the two drawing rooms, for we have quite too many people in this small room for Amy's good."

Mr. Latham and Sir Hartley kindly rose and performed the task for the widow. The panel doors were pushed back to reveal a second parlor of equal size. The centerpiece of the room was a beautiful pianoforte set before the front windows. When Mr. Latham admired the instrument, Mrs. Reed informed the party that the pianoforte had been a gift from her late father as a young girl.

Mrs. Sanford rose and went to the musical instrument to admire the workmanship. Everyone followed but Amy and Sir Hartley. While the rest of the company gathered in the other room, the baronet came and sat at the edge of Amy's sofa.

"How are you feeling, Miss Addington?" His green eyes locked with hers, and Amy felt breathless for a moment.

At last she gathered her thoughts. "I-I am quite recovered, but my aunt insists I still be treated like an invalid. She has decreed that I cannot dance at Lady Halifort's ball."

Hart gave her an understanding smile; still, he was glad he wouldn't have to worry about her being twirled about the room by some handsome gentleman while he was otherwise engaged. "I know you are disappointed, but you mustn't endanger your health."

Frustration raced through Amy. He wasn't likely to agree to let her help him if he thought her still an invalid. "You both worry too much. It is little more than a deep scratch, I do assure you."

Just then Helen began to play a tune on the pianoforte as the others stood round her listening. The pair on the sofa turned to watch her. Miss Reed owned a remarkable talent. Hart, gazing at her, noted, "She is very good."

"So she is." Amy sat in silence a moment, her mind still lingering on the subject of the ball. She returned to that subject, determined to convince Sir Hartley that she might be able to do something to help him. "I am perfectly able to dance even now, but I won't worry my aunt further by going against her wishes. I have put her through too much upheaval as it is with this accident. But I don't wish to spend all evening sitting idle against the wall listening to the dowagers gossip. I was hoping I could help you find the thief."

Hart's gaze veered back to her. "No!" The single word was emphatic as his chin jutted stubbornly.

Amy tossed back the wool rug her aunt had insisted upon, and dropped her slippered feet to the floor. "You forget I do not need your permission to stroll about Lady Halifort's rooms like any other guest."

She made to rise, but Hart's hand closed over her arm, sending an array of sensations through her.

"You are the most headstrong young lady I have ever met. Latham is right, there is no denying you when you've set your mind upon a course." Their eyes locked; then Hart's dropped to her tantalizing mouth. He found himself drawn to those kissable lips.

As if sensing his intentions, Amy huskily said, "I-I can help."

Suddenly realizing what folly he was about to commit in Mrs. Reed's drawing room, Hart straightened and struggled to return to the subject at hand. "If you insist on involving yourself, at least promise me that you will do nothing but come straight to me if you do see someone steal something."

With a mixture of disappointment and relief that Sir Hartley had remembered himself and not embarrassed them by kissing her, Amy nodded her head, making her dark curls bounce. "I promise."

"And there will be no weapons hidden in your reticule?" He arched one brow.

"Not even a small knife." Her brown eyes twinkled at him as she waggled her brows.

"Then you are welcome to stroll about with Max, Mr. Latham and me. I'm convinced the villain will be ferreted out at this ball. He won't be able to resist the marquess's collection of equine statues that Halifort amassed during his travels." Hart hoped he wouldn't regret allowing her to become involved, but then, it wasn't as if he had much choice. He would far rather know what she was up to than have her roving about and taking matters into her own hands.

"I shan't do anything dangerous at the ball. I'll merely be an added pair of watchful eyes." A wistful expression settled on her face as she turned and looked into the burning coals.

He reached over and turned her chin to face him. "I have said you may help. Why are you now so blue-deviled?" He hoped her sad mien had nothing to do with worries about Ruskin. Hart wished he could assure her that the earl would never again bother her or Miss Reed, but, having moved out of his aunt's house on the flimsiest of excuses the morning after Miss Addington's shooting, he didn't know if his cousin had gone on to London or returned to Bath.

She played with a fold in the fabric of her white gown with blue dots. " 'Tis only that this would have been my first ball, and I am not allowed to dance."

Wanting to remove the sadness from her face, Hart realized that Miss Reed was playing a waltz. He took Amy's hand. "I have an idea. Come with me."

Amy didn't protest in the least. She knew in that instant she would follow the gentleman almost anywhere.

The baronet led her to the side of the room where they could not be seen by the others, then took her in his arms. Very slowly at first they began to waltz around in a small circle. Amy was shocked at the impact of his hand holding hers, the other at her waist. It was as if she felt alive for the first time. His nearness overwhelmed her senses. Their eyes locked; then their movements grew slower and slower, until they stopped completely. The music still flowed around them, but it was as if they could no longer hear anything but the beating of their own hearts in unison.

Hart tilted her chin up and his lips covered hers, devouring her sweet, soft mouth. As the passion grew, he crushed her to him, wanting every part of her. She responded with eager innocence.

"Sir Hartley!" Mrs. Reed called from the far reaches of the other room. "Where have you gotten to, sir? You are a man of Society; come and give Helen advice on what are the best pieces to perform for a group."

Reluctantly the gentleman released Amy, ending the kiss. Drawing back, he looked into warm brown eyes that stared back with bewitched intensity. Then to his surprise, the young lady's face settled into a look of consternation, as if she'd made a startling discovery of something not very pleasant.

He wanted to assure her that he was not like Silas, that he intended to make her an offer. "Miss Addington, I love you—"

At that moment Mrs. Reed stepped into the rear parlor. "There you are. Amy, whatever are you doing up and about? You will make yourself quite ill, and then you shan't be able to go to the ball and watch the dancing."

The dazed young lady turned to her concerned relative. "I-I was feeling a bit fatigued, Aunt. If you've no objection I should like to go to my room."

"Of course you must retire if you feel the urge." Her aunt came to her. "You *are* looking a bit flushed, my dear." Mrs. Reed turned to Sir Hartley. "Go and join the others, sir. Tell them I shall return in a few moments."

As Mrs. Reed ushered her niece from the parlor, Hart berated himself for being too precipitous with Amy. He should have declared his intentions before he kissed her. After all, she'd had little evidence that the men in his family treated the women in hers with respect. Or had the mere depth of his passion frightened the innocent girl? He vowed to move more slowly with her the next time they met. With little eagerness, he joined the group round the pianoforte.

Upstairs in her room, Amy's thoughts were in turmoil as Molly removed her gown. She'd been so elated when Sir Hartley had drawn her into his arms and waltzed with her. His tantalizing kiss had awakened sensations within her that even now left her wanting more. And then her aunt's voice had penetrated her euphoria—a voice full of plots and plans as usual.

The voice again interrupted Amy's thoughts.

"Come, child, you must rest. I cannot leave Helen alone for long." Aunt Vivian stood beside Amy's bed where she'd tossed back the covers.

Bemused, Amy watched as the maid laid her gown neatly over the back of a chair. There was a sudden urge to snatch the dress up and redress, to go to Sir Hartley and declare her own love.

"Come, child, don't dawdle," Mrs. Reed said, eyeing the clock on the mantelpiece.

Without a word of protest, Amy climbed up into the bed. "I think Mrs. Sanford will watch out for Helen."

"Bah! Viola Sanford is one of my oldest friends, but she is the greatest of gossips. If Helen were to make the least misstep with one of the gentlemen, it would be repeated all over town before midnight. Besides, I've settled upon a new plan for the dear girl."

Amy grew cold as she sat on the linen sheets. She had learned to be afraid of her aunt's grand plans. "Do you not think it wiser to allow my cousin to recover from her disappointment regarding Lord Ruskin before you begin to push her at another gentleman?"

"But that is the beauty of my new plan. She is already acquainted with this gentleman. Mrs. Sanford tells me the baronet is well respected, plump in the pockets and has a large estate in Shropshire. I think Helen needs a husband who has some age and wisdom. Someone to look out for her and protect her." Aunt Vivian pulled the covers up about her niece. "Rest well, my dear. Helen and I shall see you at supper."

Without another word, Mrs. Reed hurried Molly from the room, leaving Amy tormented with guilt. Her aunt had done so much for her, bringing her and her sister from Italy, keeping her on as companion to Helen even when disaster had destroyed the lady's financial stability. How could Amy now dash the lady's hopes for an alliance between Helen and the baronet?

Helen had suffered enough disappointment due to Aunt Vivian's schemes; perhaps the best solution would be to speak with the girl and tell her the truth. The one thing that comforted Amy was that Helen had shown not the least interest in Sir Hartley. Surely she wouldn't be disappointed to find his heart already engaged. But would she be devastated to discover that the girl who was her companion had found her heart's desire long before Helen?

The old Helen might have been, but Amy didn't think the girl who'd shared her afternoons over the past few days would be upset. That Helen would surely be happy for her cousin, would she not?

Uttering a sigh, Amy turned on her side. The Minerva medallion round her neck tumbled to the pillow. She picked it up and fingered the good luck charm. She knew she loved Sir Hartley, and he had just declared his love for her. Would he risk the displeasure of his family to make her an offer of marriage? Perhaps she would have her answer on the morrow. Surely he would call and end any uncertainty on her part, as well as put an end to Aunt Vivian's newest plan.

Ten

An early resolution to Amy's dilemma with Aunt Vivian was not to come so easily. The following day Noel arrived and dashed her hopes of seeing the baronet with a whispered, "Sir Hartley has been called back to London by the Home Secretary."

Plucking at the blanket that covered her where she reclined on the daybed in the rear parlor, Amy didn't look into the young man's eyes as she inquired, "Did he send a message?"

Noel dropped into the nearest chair. "He only told me to inform you he'll return in time for the marchioness's ball."

Even as she dealt with her disappointment, Amy noted that her friend sounded utterly dejected himself. He sat slouched in the chair, his face a picture of discontent with his gaze riveted on Helen. That young lady was seated on the opposite side of the double parlors with her mother, Miss Sanford, Mrs. Sanford and that lady's newly arrived nephew, Lord Marpole. Amy knew at once that the arrival of an eligible aristocratic suitor had again dashed Noel's hopes with regard to her cousin.

Her gaze roved to the gentleman introduced to her some minutes earlier. Marpole was young, titled and well funded. The only flaw that Amy detected was his vanity, which was as obvious at the outset as his black curls. He'd positioned himself beside Helen on a green damask sofa which afforded him a full-length view of his person in a gilt-framed looking glass on the opposite side of the room. He spent almost as much time admiring his own reflection as the visage of the lady beside him. Yet for all his obvious vanity, he would still be considered an extremely eligible party. Amy could think of nothing to say that would ease her friend's pain.

Into her silence, Noel remarked, "I think I shall leave Bath once we have helped Sir Hartley apprehend his thief."

"Leave?" Amy's attention was now centered on the man across from her. "You cannot give up so soon. Why, until Helen has a ring on her finger there is always hope." She tossed the blanket aside and slid to the end of the daybed. "I cannot believe that after all Helen has experienced in this past week that she would fall for that vacuous, vain . . ." Amy searched her mind for another word that would fit the arrogant man.

"*Viscount* is the word you are looking for, my dear. The one *V* word that negates all his bad qualities, at least as far as Mrs. Reed and Helen are concerned. I saw it in their eyes the moment Mrs. Sanford introduced the man." Noel turned to gaze morosely into the fire.

Amy peered over her shoulder to where her cousin sat in conversation with the viscount. She appraised Helen's lovely features but could see nothing but polite interest in whatever the man was telling her. In her mien there was none of the excessive giggling and inane flirting that she'd displayed with Ruskin. At that exact moment, Helen glanced at Noel, and her face looked almost melancholy, but the flash of sad emotion was so brief that one would have missed it had one not been paying close attention. That look gave Amy encouragement that her young relative had learned from her mistake, and wasn't bewitched by Marpole's looks, title or money.

With a smile, Amy opened her mouth to tell Noel of her discovery. Then she stayed herself as she noted the pain on the young man's face. If she spoke, she might be giving him false hope, for she didn't know exactly what was in her cousin's heart. Only time would tell if Helen was brave enough to go against her mother's wishes.

Deciding to take another path to keep in contact with the one man who loved her cousin, Amy said, "We intend to come to London as soon as my sister returns from her honeymoon. Do give me your direction and I shall write you. You will come and call on us there, won't you?"

Noel shook his head. "I'm not going to London this Season. My uncle has invited me to his estate in Scotland, and Father thinks I should go. They seem to believe I need to learn a bit more about horses if I'm to be running a racing stable."

Not knowing what to say, Amy sat and stared into the flames. So Noel was destined to be his uncle's steward. Life was so very complicated. If only Noel had wealth, her aunt might have been willing to forgo a title, but she would never consent to her daughter marrying a man whose destiny was little better than that of an upper servant.

Rallying from her dark thoughts for Noel's sake, she took her friend's hand. "Then we shall enjoy the little time we have left together."

He looked up and gave her a sad smile, mussing his red curls in his distraction. " 'Twas my good fortune that I offered to escort you ladies to the St. Valentine's Day Ball *yesterday* and your aunt accepted." He tossed a dark look in the direction of Lord Marpole. "That is, unless the viscount convinces her to change her mind."

"Even Aunt Vivian would not do anything so improper. We shall gladly accept your escort. Besides, you and I have important matters to attend at the ball." Her eyes twinkled at the prospect of their adventure in looking for the thief, or perhaps it was the idea of again seeing the baronet that gave her such a feeling of anticipation.

The young man sat forward, showing his first animation since the viscount had entered the Reeds' drawing rooms. "Sir Hartley agreed to let you help?"

She nodded her head. "As long as I am weapon free."

Noel gave a shout of laughter.

Across the room, the sound drew the attention of the people quietly conversing on other matters. The elder ladies frowned at the pair sitting so close together beside the fire, Lord Marpole lifted his quizzing glass, and Helen's face grew pinched with discontent. She didn't see why she had to sit here and listen to this silly popinjay spout about the trials of dealing with his tailor, his family and his estate while Amy got to have a cozy conversation with Noel.

Mrs. Reed cleared her throat, and Helen dutifully struggled to smile at whatever Lord Marpole was gabbling about. Her gaze returned to the viscount's stunningly handsome face. She told herself she must not let her experience with Lord Ruskin color her judgment against other gentlemen. This titled man might improve on closer acquaintance. She'd known from the moment he'd been introduced that her mother approved, and even she had been affected by his handsome looks. With a determined effort, she set out to enchant the young viscount.

Sir Hartley tossed his greatcoat to Birdwell as he crossed the front hall of his town house in Portman

Square. Fatigue radiated in every muscle as he lifted his beaver hat from his head. But he couldn't help being pleased by the speed of his journey from Bath. He'd managed to cover the hundred-and-seven-mile trip in just under eight hours and hadn't unduly pushed any of his teams.

"Welcome back, sir. I hope your business in Bath went well."

Hart thumbed through the messages on his front table and saw little of interest. He turned to his old family retainer. "Not as well as I had hoped, but there have been some benefits to my trip." A pair of fine brown eyes invaded his thoughts. He knew his family would be as taken with Amy as he was. Then he was struck by a strange fact. There was no letter from his mother in the clutter of missives. "Has there been any news of my mother?"

"Lady Ross is in the Blue Drawing Room, sir."

"My mother is here!" Something must be wrong, Hart thought. Her plans had been set for a stay of three months, since she greatly disliked the long journey.

"She arrived two days ago, sir, inquirin' when you intended to return from your trip." Birdwell made no mention of the other prying questions the staff had fended off from the lady. He hesitated a moment, then added, "She has a guest with her. A Miss Keller, sir."

The hairs on the back of Hart's neck prickled. Was his mother once again matchmaking? There was only one way to find out. He strode up the stairs and entered the Blue Drawing Room. At the fireplace sat his mother, slender and regal in a deep purple gown. Seated opposite was a young lady who looked to be barely out of the schoolroom, her blonde hair done in an elaborate braid atop her head, an obvious attempt to make her appear older. Her clothes, while of expensive fabrics, were clearly the work of a country seamstress with a taste for frills and furbelows. His mother looked up, a look of relief on her mildly lined face. "Hart, you have come home at last."

"As you can see, I have." He leaned down and kissed her upturned cheek. "What brings you back to Town so early, Mother? I didn't expect to see you before April."

"Where are your manners, my boy? First allow me to introduce you to Miss Sylvia Keller. She is Lady Walcott's niece, and I have agreed to bring her out this Season."

Hart said all that was proper while watching a pink blush rise in the young girl's face. He didn't know what plots and plans his mother had, but clearly this green girl hadn't a clue that she was about to be offered up to him as a bride. He politely asked her several questions about the journey, but the girl could scarcely stutter out her replies.

After several minutes of stilted conversation, Lady Ross excused the girl, telling her to make ready for an outing. They must pay some afternoon calls on all her friends to introduce Sylvia to the polite world.

The door had only just closed behind Miss Keller when Lady Ross remarked, "Her father was Leonard Keller, the nabob. The girl is worth more than a hundred thousand pounds."

"How nice for her. Mother, there is something I should like to tell you before you begin using this girl for your own purposes."

Lady Ross turned toward the fire, avoiding his censuring gaze. "I don't know what you mean, Hart."

He decided not to argue with the lady. There was little point, since she owned a remarkable ability to justify her actions, especially when plotting to find him a bride. Instead he got straight to the point. "I am in love, Mother."

"Don't be vulgar, Hart. You've only met the chit. At

least pretend to court Sylvia before making such rash statements." She made a show of frowning at her son, but there was a look of hope in her eyes that she'd at last achieved her goal.

"Not with Miss Keller. I met someone in Bath, and when I return in two days' time I shall ask her to marry me."

Lady Ross found the news so shocking that she gasped and rose, facing her son. "Do I know her? How did you meet her? Who is her family?"

He took his parent by the shoulders. "The most important thing, Mother, is that I love her."

The lady's mouth puckered into a moue as if love and marriage were not to be considered in the same breath. "Since you won't tell me who she is, I can only assume she is someone dreadful and I shall not like her." Then a look of horror settled on Lady Ross's face. "If you tell me you've decided to marry an actress or some other disreputable female, I shall scream."

Hart shook his head. " 'Tis nothing like that. She comes from a noble family, but circumstances have left her having to work for a living. She is presently acting as companion to her cousin."

"A companion! After all the females I've introduced you to, you decided to fall in love with a penniless female." Lady Ross pulled free from her son's hold and began to pace back and forth. "Dukes' daughters, earls' daughters and viscounts' daughters were there for your asking, but instead you want to wed a nobody." She paced for several minutes, then stopped, shaking a finger at her son. "And what is worse, I have saddled myself with that hen-witted, milk-and-water miss to chaperon for an entire Season while you will be off on your honeymoon."

Crossing his arms, Hart looked askance at his mother. "I tried to tell you that I would find my own wife, but you wouldn't listen." A twinge of pity for her predicament tickled his conscience and he added, "Don't fret so. After all, she is a nabob's daughter. I should think you won't have any trouble firing her off."

The lady plopped down in the nearest chair in frustration. "Perhaps you are correct. But enough about Miss Keller. Tell me more about this young lady in Bath."

Hart rhapsodized about Amy's beauty and strength of character for several minutes; then spying the incredulous expression on his mother's face, he realized that she wanted the pertinent basics. As with most of Society, family connections were important to her. "Her father was the younger brother of Baron Landry. Miss Addington has lived in Italy her entire life and has only just come to England."

A thoughtful expression settled on Lady Ross's face. "I knew the current baroness years ago. At least there's respectable bloodlines if nothing else."

Hart knelt in front of his mother. "I love her, and I think she loves me, which is more important than blood or money, in my opinion."

Lady Ross looked skeptical, but at last she patted his cheek. "I have only wanted you to be happy, dear boy, and to continue the Ross line. If Miss Addington is the woman you want, then I shall do my best to love her as well. Go to Bath and fetch her to me."

He kissed his mother's hand, then rose. "I still have a matter of business to attend for the Home Secretary in Bath, Mother. I'm not likely to return to London for several weeks once I finish my meeting here with Lord Sidmouth."

His mother looked thoughtful, then smiled. "Why, I've not seen my sister in years. I shall join you in Bath. Roslyn and I shall have a comfortable coze, and you can bring round Miss Addington."

Hart drew his hands behind his back and gazed at

his mother as a chastened smile crept across his face. "There is a bit of a problem." He quickly explained that he was no longer staying with his aunt and cousin. After some hesitation, he realized there would be no keeping the truth about such a family matter from her, so he disclosed the extent of Silas's villainy toward Amy's cousin and his own role in the final resolution.

Lady Ross rocked back in her seat, stunned by what she heard, but at last she remarked, "Well, I always did think the boy dreadfully spoiled. And so I shall tell my sister if she dares to say one word against Miss Addington or her cousin."

It was Hart's turn to be surprised by his parent's total support of a woman she'd never met. He kissed his mother and told her he would bring Amy to her as soon as may be possible.

The days leading up to the Haliforts' St. Valentine's Day Ball were busy for the ladies on Forester Road. Helen was constantly being taken for drives by Lord Marpolo. Noel arrived each evening to escort Mrs. Reed and her daughter to whatever event they wished to attend, be it a private party or public concert. Amy, under orders from her aunt, stayed home and recuperated. She put her time to good use, fashioning a ball gown from some of the unused material she'd purchased before leaving Basingstoke. She was determined to look her best and took great pains with the white silk and spider gauze muslin fabric. She even ventured out one afternoon while Mrs. Reed and Helen were making calls and purchased red ribbon and small red roses. Fearful that her aunt, who'd become a bit overprotective, would object to the excursion, Amy swore Molly to silence.

Of Lord Ruskin there was no word. The ladies hoped they'd seen the last of the gentleman, at least in Bath.

In truth, as their excitement about the approaching ball grew, they gave little thought to a man now held beneath contempt.

On the morning of the fourteenth, Amy arose early with butterflies in her stomach, but she couldn't determine if it was because she was about to attend her first ball, or because she would once again see Sir Hartley that evening. Would he declare himself, or must she wait until they had captured the man who was thieving from his friends?

At least her worries about Aunt Vivian pushing her daughter at the baronet had been relieved by the appearance of Lord Marpole. His timely arrival had saved her the trouble of telling Helen that Sir Hartley had declared his love, if rather haphazardly. She was looking forward to the evening with joy.

Her one concern was Helen. Over the past several days, the girl had appeared listless and wan. Amy had tried to talk with her, but her cousin had brushed all concerns aside, saying she was only tired. While on her clandestine shopping trip with the maid, Amy had purchased new silk evening gloves as a gift, hoping to rally Helen's spirits.

The gift was to be a surprise. After giving the matter some thought, she took the present wrapped in silver paper and slipped into Helen's room. The girl lay sleeping, but Sugar raised her head and watched Amy with alert brown eyes, never making a sound. Looking about the room, she decided the best place to put the gift was in the top drawer of her cousin's dresser. That way she wouldn't find them until she dressed that evening.

Amy tiptoed to the Sheraton chest of drawers and tugged gently on the top drawer, hoping to make no noise. It held for a moment, then gave with a sudden jerk, causing the contents to shift violently. A soft thud sounded inside the rosewood furniture. Curious as to what would make such a loud noise in a drawer with only gloves and scarves, Amy lifted the material. A small jeweled swan sparkled in the recesses of the drawer. She lifted the lovely little silver bird encrusted with diamonds. Where had Helen gotten such an expensive piece?

"Whatever are you doing in my personal things?"

Amy turned to see her cousin sitting up in bed, a look somewhere between anger and fear on her face. "Helen, good morning. I came to leave you something for tonight." She hesitated a moment, then opened her hand to display the silver swan. "Where did this lovely bird come from? I should rather think it quite valuable."

Helen's face blanched white. She threw back her covers and dashed to where her cousin stood holding the swan. Yanking the silver bird from Amy's hand's, Helen snapped, "That is none of your concern. How dare you pry into my private affairs?"

Amy stood stunned by Helen's reaction. It was as if the girl had reverted to her old spoiled ways. "I'm sorry. I only meant to put this gift in your drawer."

A pink blush rose on Helen's cheeks. "I-I'm sorry. I don't mean to be rude, but you must promise not to tell Mumu about the swan."

Torn by her cousin's request, Amy hesitated. How had the girl acquired the valuable little statue? And why must it be a secret from Aunt Vivian? In a flash of memory, Amy thought of the aqua ribbon her cousin had mysteriously acquired in Basingstoke. A chill raced down her spine. Had some gentleman presented her with such an expensive token? Then an even more terrifying thought came. Was it possible that her cousin had stolen the silver swan?

Amy remembered that on the night she was shot, Sir Hartley had said there had been other robberies before he'd come to Bath. Robberies at the very routs they'd attended. Could this silver swan be one of the stolen pieces? Was it possible that Helen had been stealing things since the very beginning? Helen *had* been wandering alone at Lady Simmons's musicale. Did she have the Aphrodite statue hidden away somewhere?

The more Amy thought, the more the questions came. She had to know the truth. "Helen, you must tell me where you got this bird."

The girl blushed pink, but shook her head. "You will only be angry."

"I promise I won't."

Helen turned away from her cousin. "I-it was a gift, and I know you think I shouldn't—"

The door opened and Vivian Reed stood in the entry. "I thought I heard voices in here. Whatever are you girls doing up so early? You will be worn to the socket by the time the ball is in full swing."

Helen turned to her cousin, her eyes wide with terror that Amy would betray her. The silver bird had disappeared into the folds of her nightrail. "We were just speaking of this evening, Mama. Isn't that right, Cousin?"

Amy didn't know what to do. Her cousin might be a thief, but how could she betray her without any real evidence save that silver swan that Helen swore was a gift? Against her better judgment, Amy said, "Aunt Vivian, don't worry about us. We shall take a nap this afternoon and be fresh for the ball."

The widow's gaze moved from one girl to the other. She sensed some underlying tension, but put it down to excitement about their big evening. "Well, come along, Amy, and have some breakfast. Helen, hurry down once you are dressed. You will have all day to discuss the ball."

With a very unsettled mind, Amy followed her aunt out of the room. About to close the door, she looked back at her cousin. Helen silently mouthed the words "Thank you." Which only caused Amy more conflict. Suddenly all her joy in the ball fled. Would she be forced to unmask her cousin as the infamous Bath thief?

The one person who could relieve her fears about Helen was Sir Hartley. He would know if the silver swan was one of the missing pieces. As she followed her aunt downstairs, she prayed that the jeweled bird had never seen the inside of any house in Bath but this one.

Halifort House was a large Elizabethan manor that lay on the outskirts of Bath on the road to Bristol. In the early winter darkness, the house glowed brightly with lights, and torches lit the long front drive to welcome the members of Bath's elite to the most important social event of the winter Season.

The ladies and Noel were strangely quiet as the Latham carriage edged closer to the front stairs in the crush of vehicles. Vivian Reed occasionally uttered some inane bit of advice to her young companions.

"Remember, Amy, you must not attempt to dance. You have been looking sadly pulled today, and it might be you have overestimated your recovery. We wouldn't want to have to leave early from such an important affair."

"I shall not overdo, Aunt Vivian." Amy peered out the window hoping to see Sir Hartley's carriage. She wanted her worries about Helen put to an end, for her cousin had successfully avoided her all day.

Noel, seated beside Amy, squeezed her hand conspiratorially. "Don't fret, Mrs. Reed. Helen has promised me the first dance. After that, I shall escort Amy to one of the quieter rooms and make certain she doesn't so much as tap her slippers to the music."

The lady smiled. "I don't know what we would do without you, dear boy."

At that moment a liveried footman opened the door. They climbed down from the coach, then mounted the long marble stairs to the well-lit entrance. A cluster of footmen hurried to remove their wraps. They had scarcely begun to move with the crowd up the stairs when Mrs. Reed discovered an old friend from Norfolk and stopped to converse. She urged the young people to go on to the ballroom and not to wait for her.

Anxious to find Sir Hartley, Amy searched for the gentleman in the crush of people in the Great Hall that appeared to be filled with red roses from top to bottom. She scanned the clusters of people moving up the staircase to the ballroom, then heard her cousin gasp. She turned to see Helen gazing at the top of the stairs. Amy looked up, and her gaze froze on a gentleman staring down at them—Lord Ruskin in all his elegant splendor.

Eleven

Amy took her cousin's hand, feeling a tremor race up the girl's arm. Before she could say a word, however, Noel appeared at Helen's side. "Have no fear, Miss Reed. We shall protect you from that scoundrel."

Helen blinked several times as if she couldn't believe her eyes; then her shoulders straightened and her jaw jutted defiantly. She drew her gaze from the earl to Noel. "I shan't let His Lordship ruin my evening. I believe that the first dance is yours, sir." It took a bit of effort, but at last she managed a smile.

Mr. Latham winked at her. "That's a good girl." He then offered each lady his arm. "We must find your cousin a seat before we take our position."

As Amy placed her hand on the gentleman's sleeve, she looked up to where Ruskin had stood, but thankfully he was gone. With any luck, her cousin would not be forced to speak to the blackguard all evening, for it was clear by the crush on the stairs that most of Bath Society was present.

Progress to the ballroom was slow, but soon they reached the receiving line, meeting Lady Halifort, the marquess and their daughter, a petite redhead barely out of the schoolroom. The enormous ballroom sparkled with candlelight and was bedecked with red ribbons and huge bouquets of roses. The rumor of the ball said there was no longer a hothouse rose left in the surrounding counties. The elegant chamber was everything two young ladies at their first dress ball could hope for.

After several bedazzled moments, Amy began to search the crowd for Sir Hartley's tall form. To her disappointment, there was still no sign of the baronet in the rapidly filling room. She worried he might have been delayed in Town. Or had the Home Secretary turned the matter of the thief over to someone else, since the gentleman had had no success?

A single chord of a minuet filled the ballroom, announcing that dancing was to begin. Lady Anne, the marquess's daughter, was led to the head of the set by her proud father. The guests streamed onto the floor to take their places. Noel got Amy comfortably settled near the door, since Miss Sanford was nowhere to be found, then led Helen to the floor. For just a moment Amy experienced a twinge of longing to be twirled about the parquet floor with the others; then she remembered that she had no time for regrets. Watching her beautiful cousin smile up into Noel's face, she prayed that her suspicions about Helen were false. Then she realized that hasty judgment had allowed her to make a wrong assumption about the baronet. She wouldn't do that again. Until Sir Hartley told her otherwise, she would assume that the thief was still out there and not in the arms of Noel Latham.

For a brief time Amy was content to sit and watch the dancers perform the graceful moves of the dance. She spied Lord Ruskin on the opposite side of the room dancing with a beautiful woman of questionable years. She hoped he'd at last set his sights on someone else.

As she noted the number of people not dancing, it suddenly occurred to her that the thief might already be about his dastardly business. She didn't need Noel to take her around the rooms to keep watchful eyes on those who chose not to dance. She rose and made her way to a second doorway that opened on the hall, a long corridor that appeared endless in the huge old manor. Across the way she could see that a card room had been set up to amuse many of the older guests who no longer cared about dancing. A quick survey of the chamber told her that everything had been removed from the room save the card tables and chairs. She strolled down the hall, nodding politely to people, drawing as little attention to herself as possible.

She came to a small room with a carved placard above the door designating the chamber The Horse Room. Curious, she stepped in to discover a veritable sea of horse images in every shape, size, material and medium from painting to sculpture. Standing foursquare in the center of the room was a sculpted life-size white Arabian with head arched and mane flowing. It was the kind of piece one expected to find in a garden, not indoors. Her gaze moved on to the rows and rows of statues that lined the wall. Most of the art pieces, while unique and expensive, were too large to secrete on one's person. Unfortunately, mingled with the larger pieces were small horse sculptures which might easily be taken. Seeing the sparkle of jewels on the artwork, Amy suspected this was where they were likely to find the culprit.

There were several couples in the room admiring His Lordship's collection. Amy spied a lone gentleman on the opposite side of the room, but was only able to see his silk stockings and black buckled pumps due to the great plaster horse in the middle of the room. Her heart began to race as she willed herself to move at a sedate pace around the head of the horse. To her utter surprise, she discovered an old acquaintance holding a pair of small bronzed horses fashioned in the throes of a heated race. Had she discovered the thief?

"Lord Malcolm?"

The slender young man looked up, then smiled upon seeing who beckoned him. "Why, Miss Addington, you are looking in the best of health."

"I am well, sir, but surprised to see you here." Her gaze moved to the beautifully cast statue in the gentleman's hands.

"My Uncle Halifort told me he'd just purchased this piece from a fellow near Ascot. Ain't it spectacular? As close to real life as possible." He held the small sculpted horses for her to see. There wasn't the least nervousness or guile on the young man's face.

Relief flooded over Amy. "I fear I had forgotten you were the marquess's nephew. You must come to visit often." He would have had any number of opportunities to steal were he the thief.

The young man nodded his head. "Uncle shares my love of fine prads, as you can see." Lord Malcolm swept his free hand about the room. "Of course, I prefer a real living horse, but I must say this room is a fitting monument to these magnificent creatures."

Realizing she needed to move along, Amy inquired, "Do you not intend to dance this evening, sir?"

The gentleman put down the statue he'd been admiring and turned to take Amy's hand. "Miss Addington, I am devastated. I met Mrs. Reed in the Great Hall as I entered. She tells me you are not to dance this evening. I came all the way here so that I might waltz with you." His mouth arched downward.

Amy suddenly remembered all her flirting with the gentleman at Charlcomb to keep him in the church and his subsequent interest in her. Whatever was she to do to convince him she viewed him as a mere friend? "I fear my aunt has forbade me, Lord Malcolm. Like you, I have been recently felled by illness."

The young heir to Lord Holmsby nodded; then exasperation flitted across his face when his gaze moved behind Amy. Turning, she spied Lady Anne making for them.

"There you are, Mally. I knew I would find you lurking here among my father's steeds. You promised to dance the cotillion with me." The young lady dimpled up at her tall cousin.

Perhaps it was woman's intuition, but Amy knew in an instant that the girl was mad for Lord Malcolm, and the feckless young man hadn't a clue. But even he couldn't resist Anne's warm charm and at last he smiled back. But he appeared to hesitate as he looked back at Amy, so she shooed him onward. "Do go and enjoy the ball. I want to admire Lord Halifort's collection a bit more."

Malcolm thrust out his arm to Lady Anne. "Oh, come on then, brat. Pray excuse me, Miss Addington, but duty calls."

Amy smiled for a moment as she watched the pair depart. Within minutes the room emptied of guests, so she continued her inspection of the upstairs rooms of the Haliforts' mansion that were open to the public. Perhaps it was that it was too early, or that none of the guests had yet grown tired, but most of the elaborate drawing rooms stood empty.

Deciding to widen her search, Amy wandered down the staircase to the Great Hall where people still milled about. She peered in several rooms that had small clusters of guests, but saw nothing suspicious. About to return to the upstairs where most of the guests were gathered, she spied Sir Hartley and Colonel Hensley entering the front double doors, handing their cloaks to the footmen. Her heart seemed to jump as her gaze locked on the baronet. He was very handsome in his evening clothes, the white of his cravat making him look ruggedly tan.

She hurried to greet the gentlemen. "Good evening, Colonel, Sir Hartley."

"Amy." The baronet stepped forward and took her hands, heedless of the curious eyes of the nearby guests. "You look ravishing." He drew her gloved hands to his mouth and placed a lingering kiss on the back of each.

She suddenly felt as if she couldn't breathe as she stared into his mesmerizing green eyes. She wanted to be alone with this man, not at a crowded ball.

The pair stood as if there were no one in their world but the other until the colonel cleared his throat. When Amy looked at the former soldier, there was a knowing smile on his face, and she felt her own cheeks warm.

"As my friend here has so ardently demonstrated, we are delighted to see you here, Miss Addington. But you two won't find a thief gazing into one another's eyes. Shall we spread out and begin our vigil?" Colonel Hensley looked about. "This place is enormous. You should have recruited all your friends."

Sir Hartley scanned the large Great Hall. "Constable Baker is supposed to have put several of his men here tonight disguised as footmen, so we have more people watching than just us. You start with the right side of the lower rooms, I'll take the left." The baronet then returned his gaze to Amy as Maxwell Hensley strode off. "Are you here with your cousin and aunt?"

Amy nodded, visually drinking in every line of his handsome face.

The baronet's voice lowered and his tone softened. "I have a very important question to ask later."

Amy's knees grew weak at the look in the gentleman's eyes. She had little doubt what the question would be. She would at last be able to tell her aunt and her cousin of her love. As Helen popped into Amy's mind, she suddenly remembered she needed to ask about the earlier robberies. Fear made her palms moist at what she might learn. "You said there had been earlier robberies. Do you know what was stolen?"

"I believe a jeweled dagger was taken from Lord Rowland's, and some type of bird statue from Lady Whitford's. I have the descriptions written down back at the inn."

The baronet's brows drew together in thought or puzzlement at her odd response to his statement. She took a step back as the room seemed to spin before her eyes.

"Are you feeling ill, my dear? I knew you shouldn't have come out so soon after your—"

"No, no, I am well." Amy put a hand to her head. She couldn't fall apart. Her aunt would need her once the truth was revealed. "I want to help. But first I must go and see Aunt Vivian or she will be anxious."

Worry filled the baronet's eyes. "Are you sure you are well enough, my love?"

She gave him a dazzling smile, but the effort was draining. "I am fine." With that, she turned and hurried up the marble staircase, her mind in a jumble about what to do. She stopped at the top landing, then turned and looked down at Sir Hartley who stood watching her with concern from below. Would he make her an offer of marriage once the truth was revealed? She only prayed that his love could overcome the revelations of tonight. She gave him a wave, then turned and walked blindly down the hall toward the ballroom.

Just before she reached the arched doors, she stopped to gather her thoughts. If Helen was guilty, perhaps she could give back everything and the matter could be hushed up. But what had caused her beautiful cousin to become a thief? Had her mother's loss of funds affected the girl's mind? Or had she always had a penchant for taking small items?

Amy bit at her lip. She knew she could stand here

asking herself questions all night, but until she spoke with Helen, nothing would be known.

Driven by fear, Amy stepped to the ballroom door and scanned the crowd, but in the crush of people she realized she would never find her cousin. She stepped back to the quiet of the hallway, and stood lost in thought about all the people this dreadful news would effect. Several late guests appeared at the head of the stairs, and Amy turned to move along the passageway.

Then she caught a glimpse of the skirts of her cousin's ball gown as the girl disappeared into a room at the far end of a hall. She was certain it was Helen, for she recognized the rouleau and pink roses that trimmed the hem of her gown. Did her cousin intend to steal again?

Amy moved as quickly as she could down the hall, not wanting to draw attention to herself. Her eyes remained riveted on the door through which Helen had disappeared. When she reached the portal, she stopped and took a deep breath. She reached out a trembling hand and pushed downward on the brass handle, opening the door with quiet stealth.

The scene before Amy left her frozen in shock. Helen was in the arms of Lord Ruskin, trying to fight off his unwanted advances. In a voice choked with fear, the beauty cried, "Stop, you beast. I know what you want, and I shan't let you ruin me."

"My beautiful dove, you will be mine," Ruskin murmured huskily as he pressed the girl backward on the arm of a chair, all the while pressing hot kisses on the white expanse of soft mounds exposed above the edge of her bodice.

Rage filled Amy. What would it take to end this man's obsession with her cousin? In the flash of an eye, she yanked up a vase filled with roses. She stepped up behind the earl and crashed the vase, contents and all, over the man's head.

Water, roses and shattered pottery flew about, but thankfully the earl's body protected her cousin. Startled and dazed, Lord Ruskin fell sideways to the floor into the heap of scattered roses and broken porcelain. Helen threw herself into her cousin's arms and began to weep. Her blond curls were mussed, and several of the pink roses Amy had worked into the girl's tresses hung loose.

"Stand up, you cad." Amy snapped.

Ruskin struggled to sit up, a growing lump on the side of his head. "Are you mad, woman? I should have you arrested."

The man straightened and lifted his hand to feel the tender spot. From beneath his jacket an object tumbled to the Aubusson carpet. It was a small jade statue of a horse. Amy gasped at the significance of what she was seeing. "You are the Bath thief, Lord Ruskin!"

The announcement was so shocking that Helen ceased to cry and stared at the earl with horror. "An earl a common thief?"

Ruskin was on his feet in an instant. He dashed to the wall and pulled free a small sword on display. He pointed it at the women, who clung together in fear. "Miss Addington, you have been a thorn in my side from the day we met. I've a good mind to use this blade on you and take my beautiful Helen with me."

The blood ran cold in Amy's veins. She prayed that Sir Hartley or the colonel might find them. To her amazement, Helen proved to have more pluck than Amy had ever thought.

"Do you think I would go with you without screaming to all who might hear that you had hurt my dear cousin? You are quite mad, my lord."

The earl's eyes narrowed for a moment; then an evil smile settled on his lips. "I suppose I must stick with accumulating only works of art, for you, my dear Miss Reed, have required far too much effort to acquire." He stopped and looked about, then walked to a small door that he yanked open. It was a room for storage. "Ladies, come this way." He gestured with the blade.

"What are you going to do with us?" Amy stared back defiantly.

"I collect beautiful *objets d'art,* Miss Addington, I am not a murderer. At least not yet. But I must admit, for you I might make an exception." His eyes held a rather crazed glow for a moment; then he shook his head. "I won't risk the gallows even for you. I intend to lock you in this room so that I might leave unmolested."

The girls exchanged a wary look, then edged past him into the small closet. They held their breath as the earl stepped into the confined space, but he merely took Helen's chin and turned her face toward the light. "Such a pity I cannot possess such beauty." With that, he tried to kiss her, but she turned her face away and moved into Amy's arms. He shrugged, and plucked one of the dangling pink roses from her hair. "I must have a token of our final meeting, my beauty."

He tucked the flower in his lapel, then stepped out of the room, shutting the door. The click of the lock echoed loudly in the small room as Helen wept and clung to her cousin.

"Don't worry. We shall soon be found." Amy searched her mind for a subject to take Helen's thoughts off their predicament. She suddenly realized that all her fears about her cousin had proven false. Still, she wondered where the silver swan came from. "Helen, may I ask you something?"

The girl gave a sniffling sigh, then asked, "What do you want to know?"

"Where did the diamond swan in your drawer come from?"

"What does that matter now? We might be locked in here for days in a manor this large."

Amy gave an embarrassed laugh, glad that her cousin couldn't see her face in the darkness. "That won't happen. Noel and Sir Hartley will be looking for us long before then. As to the swan, the truth is that when I saw it, I thought you were the Bath thief."

"What?" Helen's voice was full of indignation. "Me, a thief?"

"One could only wonder, when all the things taken were small and that swan is very expensive. I thought—"

Helen began to laugh. "Why, it's only silver plate and paste stone, Amy." There was a moment of silence; then the girl continued. "Do you remember I told you about a young clerk in my father's office who showed an interest in me. It was a gift from him all those years ago. It was the best he could afford at the time. I didn't want my mother to know, because she was so devastated on learning about our innocent flirtation, and she forbade me ever to speak or even think of him again."

Amy bit at her lip a moment, then asked, "Did you love him?"

A soft sigh echoed in the darkness before Helen replied. "I don't think so, but he was the first man who told me I was beautiful and he was very kind. The swan is very pretty for all that it's nearly worthless, but I never think of that young man much anymore." She gave a sigh, then added, "I haven't had much luck in finding the right man."

Amy's fingers closed around the gold charm at her neck. Perhaps it was foolish to believe that the lucky charm had helped her to find her true love, but if it did hold such powers, she hoped its magic could be shared with her cousin. She leaned over and kissed Helen's tear-dampened cheek. "Perhaps you have learned something from your experiences with Lord Ruskin. You must look for love with your heart."

Silence reigned in the small, dark space. Then Helen asked, "Do you think they will find us soon?"

Amy hoped that her comment would eventually provoke some thought about love on her cousin's part, but at present all the girl appeared to be thinking about was being rescued. Then she smiled with confidence in the darkness. Sir Hartley would find them once he realized they were missing; there wasn't the least doubt in her mind.

Hart was worried. Something was bothering Amy, and she hadn't told him what. He gazed round the Great Hall, but the cavernous room remained nearly empty of guests, as it had been since he'd arrived. Coming to a quick decision, he strode to where he'd last seen Max. Entering a large drawing room, he spied the colonel lounging with elan against the wall watching two couples who were very interested in Halifort's paintings, or were using an interest in artwork as an excuse to have some time away from the crowded ballroom.

"Max, there are so few people downstairs, I'll leave you and go help Amy keep a vigil upstairs." The baronet didn't wait for a response, but turned and hurried away.

An amused smile settled on the colonel's face as he watched his friend disappear up the stairs. "Cupid has found his mark with you, my old friend."

Upstairs, Hart scanned the long hallway but saw no sign of Amy. Thinking to find her in the ballroom, he moved to the arched doorway, but before he entered, he encountered Noel. "Have you seen Miss Addington, Latham?"

The red-haired young man shook his head and turned

back to again scan the crowd even as he spoke. "She was supposed to wait until I finished my dance with Helen; then we were to stroll about together. I have searched from one end of the ballroom to the other. She's not in there, and now I cannot find Helen either."

"Hopefully, they are together and have only gone to the ladies' retiring room." Hart took Noel's arm and maneuvered him down the hall as a large group of giggling young ladies exited the ballroom for just that destination.

Yet Noel appeared to take little comfort at the baronet's suggestion. "Did you know that Lord Ruskin is at the ball, sir?"

Sir Hartley stopped dead in his tracks. What could Silas be up to now? Why had he come back to Bath? "I had no idea. Did you speak with him?"

"No, but here he comes now." Noel gestured to the far end of the hall; then a look of relief washed over his face. "Thankfully, the ladies are nowhere in sight."

The Earl of Ruskin came striding down the hall with a purposeful step. He appeared distracted, adjusting the set of his clothes. He had yet to see the pair of gentlemen who stood against the wall observing him. Hart stepped into his cousin's path. He noted that Silas looked less than his usual fastidious self. His blond hair lay flat, appearing wet in patches, and his cravat was a wilted mess. When his gaze settled on Sir Hartley's grim countenance, the earl's face twisted into a hard, resentful mask.

"Remove yourself from my path, Cousin."

Before Hart could respond, Noel gasped, then lunged at the earl. He grabbed the man's lapels, stripping the small pink rosebud from its position. "Where did you come by this rose, you blackguard?"

A sneer tipped the earl's mouth. "Why, I believe it

was a token from a lady who willingly offered me her kisses."

Hoping to avoid a scandalous scene there in the hallway, Hart stepped between Latham and the earl, pushing his cousin back a step. As his hand touched his cousin's jacket, he felt a hard lump beneath the black superfine. An alarm went off in Hart's mind. Why would his cousin be carrying something under his coat other than money? Clearly, what he'd felt wasn't a coin pouch. Determined to find out what the man had hidden, the baronet grabbed the earl's arm and pulled him into the nearby empty drawing room. The red silk moire paper and red damask chairs created the illusion of stepping into Hades, but the men were too intent on their conversation to pay much heed to the decor.

"What do you think you are doing, Hartley?" Lord Ruskin snapped angrily as he tugged his arm free.

Without answering, Hart yanked open the earl's evening jacket and saw a bit of a swirled green and white jade statue sticking out of a hidden pocket in his cousin's jacket. He plucked the small horse free. In that instant he knew that it was his cousin who'd been stealing from his friends. But *why* was a complete mystery, since the young man had money to burn. Angrily, Hart held up the carved steed in front of his cousin's face. "I believe you are caught at last, Cousin."

"Give that back! It's mine." Silas reached for the figurine, but Hart held it away from him and grabbed the fabric of the earl's white waistcoat.

"Yours?" Hart shook his cousin slightly. "What, is it your lucky horse statue that you take to all social gatherings?"

Silas's eyes seemed to glaze over as he stared at the intricately carved statue. "It's so beautiful, I must have it if only for a short while."

Hart saw a hint of desperation in his cousin's face at

that moment that truly frightened him, and he released his hold on his waistcoat. It was as if the earl's desire to possess the statue was a physical need, or more like a sickness. "Only for a while, Silas?"

The earl nodded his head. "Mother has Waxford search my rooms regularly. Whenever they find one of my . . . treasures, they always see that it's returned." Ruskin's blue gaze never moved from the jade horse. "It's strange, but after several weeks, the magic that entices me to take it leaves."

Stunned to find that his aunt knew of her son's problem, Hart didn't know what to say. He knew the lady would be destroyed if Silas was exposed to all of Society. He looked to Latham and saw the pity on the young man's face. It was clear that Silas had some obsession that bordered on lunacy. Yet what could they do? It wasn't as if he had truly harmed anyone, for his aunt made certain that all the stolen items were eventually returned. But they couldn't let things continue.

While lost in momentary thought, Hart's gaze fell to the pink rose clutched in Noel's hand. A disturbing thought took hold. "Silas, where is Miss Reed?"

The earl's face took on a dreamy quality. "I want to possess her as well." Then his golden looks were marred by a pronounced frown and his eyes focused directly on his cousin. "You and Miss Addington ruined that as well. I lured Miss Reed from the ballroom, but she wouldn't even let me have a token kiss to say goodbye . . . so I took one of her roses."

"Where are Miss Reed and Amy?" Hart took a step forward, his hand tightening around the jade figurine.

Silas arched one blond brow quizzically. "What do you intend to do now that you know the truth, Cousin?"

"I shall draw your cork at present unless you tell me what you have done with the ladies."

The earl paled and straightened. "There is no need

for violence. They are unharmed. I locked them in a small storage room just off the Gold Drawing Room at the end of the hall."

Latham turned and left the room immediately, leaving Hart to deal with his cousin. Hart eyed the earl for a moment, then realized that any plans would have to be discussed with his aunt. "Go home, Silas. Is your mother at the ball?"

Ruskin nodded his head.

"Then find her and give her some excuse. Don't touch anything. Walk straight downstairs and call for your carriage. You can tell her the truth tonight, or you can wait until I come in the morning, but she will be told that you have been stealing here in Bath."

For the first time, Silas's face took on the look of a frightened six-year-old. "I'd rather go back home to Lincolnshire."

"You may, once all has been untangled here and all the things you stole returned. In fact, I should think you might want to stay at the castle until Lord Sidmouth can be convinced not to pursue a case against you."

Lord Ruskin looked truly frightened, but he did as his cousin bade him. He left Sir Hartley without another word.

Hart followed his cousin to the hall door and watched the man hurry toward the ballroom as if he had demons at his heels. Perhaps he did. What else would cause a man of wealth to steal what he could easily afford to buy? The mind was truly a mystery.

Then Hart remembered Amy was locked in a room with Miss Reed. He turned and hurried to the room that Silas had designated as their prison. When he stepped into the Gold Drawing Room, he discovered Noel with a fireplace poker in his hand about to batter the Haliforts' storage room door.

"Wait!" Hart called.

Noel's arm froze with the poker held high. He looked over his shoulder, calling, "The door's locked and I cannot find the key."

"Did you look in all these vases and bowls sitting about the room?" Hart began to look in the decorative displays on each table.

Tossing the poker to the rug, Noel stepped to the door and called, "We are looking for the key, ladies. It will only be a few moments more."

After inspecting many possible hiding places for the key, Hart's gaze fell to the shattered vase of roses in the middle of the room. Then he turned to the remaining vase that sat on a table next to the storage room door. "Noel, come help a moment."

Hart picked up the vase. "Take the flowers out."

The young man frowned as he looked at the thorny roses, but did as he was urged. Using both hands, he gently lifted the entire dripping arrangement free from the gold leaf vase. Hart turned and poured the remaining contents into a porcelain bowl painted with people from George the First's era. There was a slight clink as the key tumbled into the bowl.

"We have the key, ladies," Hart called, while Noel heedlessly tossed the roses beside the empty vase.

The key easily slid into the lock, and the door opened to find two beautiful and grateful young ladies. Without a word, Amy stepped out of the small, dark room into Hart's arms. "Did Silas hurt you?"

Amy smiled up at him. "No. He threatened to, but whatever his madness, he's not dangerous."

After a moment's hesitation, Miss Reed dashed out of the room and threw herself into Noel's arms, to the surprise of that young man. "Oh, my dearest Noel, I am delighted to see your darling face again."

A smile lit up the young man's round countenance, and he grinned over his love's mussed blond curls at

Sir Hartley and Amy, who stood bemused by Helen's conduct. After savoring the moment, he tilted up the girl's chin. "Glad enough to consent to be my wife?"

Helen threw her arms about his neck. "I will. I don't care that you have no money or title. I realized tonight on the dance floor that you are the one I love, and I shall tell Mama just that." She looked back over her shoulder at Amy. "You will help me convince Mama I love Noel, won't you, Amy?"

"I shall."

Noel threw back his head and laughed. After he got his glee under control, he realized the others were looking at him as if he were demented. "I don't think that should be as difficult as you think."

Helen took a step back. "My dear Noel, you know that Mama is determined—"

"I know, my love. I have known from the first day I met you and your mama that you both had a plan. That is why I deliberately didn't tell you much about myself. A man don't want to be taken for his money and station. He wants his wife to adore him as he does her." Noel traced a finger along Helen's delicate jaw. "Especially a man with few looks to attract a beautiful woman."

"Don't say that," Helen said, stepping into Noel's arms. "I adore your smile and your kindness."

Amy looked up at Hart, who smiled and shrugged as if to say all this was news to him as well. She looked back to where Helen stood hugging the man she loved. "Are you telling us, Noel, that you have prospects?"

Noel grinned. "My father is the younger brother and heir of the Earl of Kilgallan. My uncle and his wife weren't blessed with children, so eventually I shall inherit his lands and title." He tilted Helen's chin up. "Shall we go and tell your mother that some day you shall be a countess as my wife?"

"A countess?" Helen repeated numbly, so stunned was she at the turn of events, but she allowed Noel to lead her away.

Hart's arm tightened around Amy, who, like her cousin, was amazed. "Did you know about Noel's expectations?"

"I don't want to talk about Noel and Miss Reed. I want to tell you that I adore you."

Amy's cheeks blushed pink, but she looked lovingly into his eyes. "And I love you."

"Enough to marry me in the morning at Bath Abbey?" Hart devoured her with his eyes as he drew her into his arms.

"W-what about the banns?" Amy's body molded to the hard, muscular man, her heart pounding with excitement.

"While I was in London I purchased a Special License. Can you be ready in the afternoon? We shall be wed and on our way to London, if you want."

Hart's mouth closed over Amy's, and she had no opportunity to say yea or nay for some minutes. When at last the gentleman drew back before passion took them too far, Amy asked in a breathless little voice, "What was the question, Sir Hartley?"

In a husky voice Hart repeated, "Will you marry me on the morrow, my love?"

"Yes, please, Sir Hartley." Amy slid her arms around the gentleman's neck.

He kissed her nose. "Call me Hart, my love."

Amy's brown eyes twinkled up at him as she dimpled. "Why, for the very first time I have received a Hart for St. Valentine's Day."

"You, my love, have a Hart for all time." With that, he drew her into his arms and kissed her passionately.

* * *

The ceremony took place the following afternoon at Bath Abbey. That was the earliest Sir Hartley could end his business with Constable Baker, whose questions about the thief were left mostly unanswered. The stolen items were recovered from where the earl had secreted them at Laura Place and were given to Mr. Baker to return to their owners with whatever explanation he chose.

To Amy's surprise, Lady Ruskin and a very subdued earl were in attendance at the wedding. Her Ladyship made the terse announcement that she and her son were going abroad for a while, along with the curate from the village church back home. No prying questions were asked; Amy merely recommended they not miss Tuscany or Rome.

A beaming Mrs. Reed, Helen and her fiancé, Mr. Latham, escorted the bride to the cathedral. Amy's aunt had been perfectly agreeable to her niece's choice of a small wedding, for, after all, Vivian had a much larger affair to plan for her daughter.

After the ceremony, Colonel Hensley kissed the bride and promised to come for a visit once they returned from their wedding trip. Aunt Vivian wept as she bade her niece to have a safe journey. Helen and Noel scarcely managed to take their eyes from one another long enough to bid the newlyweds Godspeed.

The carriage traveled northward at a sedate pace so that Sir Hartley and his bride could enjoy the journey. "We go only as far as Marlborough tonight, my love. I have arranged for us to stay at an inn there. Then on to London, where I must report to Lord Sidmouth. Then wherever you want to go, I shall take you."

Amy fingered the gold buttons on her husband's waistcoat. "Would you think it strange if I told you I didn't want to leave England? I've seen quite enough of the world. I should like to see the land of my father."

Hart tilted her head up and kissed her mouth. "Not strange at all. I have a small hunting box in Northumberland. While I attend my business in London, I shall send Birdwell ahead to open the house and make it ready for us. I shall show you as much of England as you should like to see before we settle at Ross Manor."

"That sounds wonderful."

Hart couldn't seem to take his eyes off his beautiful new wife. His gaze lit upon the gold medallion which lay nestled between her breasts. His fingers brushed her soft skin as he lifted it, unknowingly sending a wave of sensations through her. "Tell me about this necklace that you always wear."

"Oh, I had quite forgotten the charm. Will you undo the clasp?" She sat up and turned around. As he worked with the chain, she told him the story of Alexander's gift to his sisters before he left them in Rome eight years ago. She turned around, and Hart dropped the good luck charm into her open hand. "Do you think I could meet Lady Margaret, Countess of Wotherford, while we are in London?"

"The dowager? Whatever for?" Hart asked the question, but his mind appeared to be on his bride as he ran his hands up her arms and tugged her to him.

"She is our godmother. I am certain Alexander will come to her first when he returns to England. I want her to give him the good luck charm." Amy smiled as she once again melted into his embrace.

Hart kissed her ear. "You may see whomever you want in London, my love, as long as you spend your nights with me."

Amy smiled. "I am yours forever, my Hart. But we must make certain that my brother receives the medallion, for I want him to find his heart's desire, just as Adriana and I found ours."

"As you wish, my love." With that, Sir Hartley and

Lady Ross put aside thoughts of good luck charms and brothers to surrender themselves to their passion, or as much as possible until they reached the privacy of an inn.

ABOUT THE AUTHOR

Lynn Collum lives with her family in Florida. She is the author of six Zebra Regency romances and is currently working on her seventh, THE WEDDING CHARM, to be published in April 2001. Lynn loves hearing from readers and you may write to her c/o Zebra Books. Please include a self-addressed stamped envelope if you wish a response.

BOOK YOUR PLACE ON OUR WEBSITE AND MAKE THE READING CONNECTION!

We've created a customized website just for our very special readers, where you can get the inside scoop on everything that's going on with Zebra, Pinnacle and Kensington books.

When you come online, you'll have the exciting opportunity to:

- View covers of upcoming books

- Read sample chapters

- Learn about our future publishing schedule (listed by publication month *and author*)

- Find out when your favorite authors will be visiting a city near you

- Search for and order backlist books from our online catalog

- Check out author bios and background information

- Send e-mail to your favorite authors

- Meet the Kensington staff online

- Join us in weekly chats with authors, readers and other guests

- Get writing guidelines

- AND MUCH MORE!

**Visit our website at
http://www.zebrabooks.com**

More Zebra Regency Romances

Merlin's Legacy

A Series From
Quinn Taylor Evans

__**Daughter of Fire** $5.50US/$7.00CAN
  0-8217-6052-1

__**Daughter of the Mist** $5.50US/$7.00CAN
  0-8217-6050-5

__**Daughter of Light** $5.50US/$7.00CAN
  0-8217-6051-3

__**Dawn of Camelot** $5.50US/$7.00CAN
  0-8217-6028-9

__**Shadows of Camelot** $5.50US/$7.00CAN
  0-8217-5760-1

Call toll free **1-888-345-BOOK** to order by phone or use this coupon to order by mail.

Name _____

Address _____

City _____ State _____ Zip _____

Please send me the books I have checked above.

I am enclosing $_____

Plus postage and handling* $_____

Sales tax (in New York and Tennessee) $_____

Total amount enclosed $_____

*Add $2.50 for the first book and $.50 for each additional book.

Send check or money order (no cash or CODs) to:

Kensington Publishing Corp., 850 Third Avenue, New York, NY 10022

Prices and Numbers subject to change without notice.

All orders subject to availability.

Check out our website at **www.kensingtonbooks.com**